'Engaging and entertaining.'
Independent on Sunday

'An **adventure** of old-fashioned charm.'
Sunday Times

'Perfect for **captivating** the imagination.'
Mumsnet

'**Absorbing**… brimming with atmospheric detail.'
Carousel

'My go-to author for historical fiction.'
The Bookbag

'Rich in **thrilling** details.'
Lovereading4kids

'Compelling.'
Metro

'Absorbing, sensitive and **genuinely magical** in feel.'
Independent

'A fast, exciting read.'
The School Librarian

'your middle grade kids (ages 8-12) haven't discovered
Emma Carroll yet, then they're **missing out.**'
Irish Times

'Beautiful.'
Luna's Little Library

By the Same Author

Frost Hollow Hall
The Girl Who Walked on Air
In Darkling Wood
The Snow Sister
Strange Star
Letters from the Lighthouse

About the Author

Emma Carroll was a secondary school English teacher before leaving to write full time. She has also worked as a news reporter, an avocado picker and the person who punches holes into Filofax paper. She graduated with distinction from Bath Spa University's MA in Writing For Young People. *Secrets of a Sun King* is Emma's eighth novel. She lives in the Somerset hills with her husband and two terriers.

SECRETS
OF A
SUN · KING

Emma Carroll

ff

FABER & FABER

First published in 2018
by Faber & Faber Limited
Bloomsbury House,
74–77 Great Russell Street,
London WC1B 3DA

Typeset by MRules
Printed by CPI Group (UK) Ltd, Croydon CR0 4YY

© Emma Carroll, 2018

The right of Emma Carroll to be identified as author
of this work has been asserted in accordance with Section 77
of the Copyright, Designs and Patents Act 1988

A CIP record for this book
is available from the British Library

ISBN 978-0-571-32849-9

FSC
www.fsc.org
MIX
Paper from
responsible sources
FSC® C101712

8 10 9 7

For Karl, the sort of friend
I count as family

PART ONE

LONDON, NOVEMBER 1922

With intense excitement, I drew back the bolts.

HOWARD CARTER, ARCHAEOLOGIST

1

One filthy wet Wednesday morning, the world stopped making sense. I wish I could say I'd been expecting it, like those clever people who smell thunderstorms or feel tidal waves before they hit, but that wasn't quite how it happened.

We'd been eating breakfast, Mum and me, bumping knees under our tiny kitchen table as we polished off the last of the bread and dripping. I'd be hungry again within the hour: I always was. I was also dreading school. So you could say the day had started as grim as any other. Until, that was, I saw the headline in the morning paper:

'HUMAN FEET FOUND IN BLOOMSBURY TOWN HOUSE.'

'Is it *true*?' I asked, baffled.

Mum was scanning the inside pages for the death notices and horoscopes, which were the bits she always read first. 'Is what true, pet?'

I pointed to the article: 'Can I see?' because it was

just the sort of queer story that'd stick in my head all day if I didn't read it.

Mum turned to the front page with a frown.

'Your dad wouldn't think much of you filling your brain with this, Lil,' she said, once she'd read it herself.

No, he probably wouldn't.

Dad wanted his daughter to be quiet, hard-working, with her nose always in a textbook. And I *was* like this, but I could be fierce if I had to be and wasn't good at niceties or looking neat for school. Which was why when Mum cut my hair off with the dressmaking scissors, Dad didn't object. Better a daughter with boy-short hair than one whose plaits were always unravelling.

Meanwhile, across the kitchen table, Mum was still holding the newspaper.

'Oh come on, let me. Dad's not even here,' I pointed out.

He'd gone to work early, as usual, selling carpets door to door. Mum said he was lucky to have a job when, since the war, times were hard for everyone. She worked in Woolworths, and no amount of lipstick could hide how tired she always looked. But at least we had a roof over our heads – a sloping attic one, because our rooms were on the very top floor, which was all right until you needed the privy. Then you'd have to go down four flights of stairs to the back yard, where you'd pray you'd remembered to bring lav paper, and that there weren't any rats waiting to nip you.

'Imagine being in the trenches, then,' Bobby Fitzpatrick, who lived in the ground-floor flat, used to say. 'The Frenchie rats were bigger than baby pigs, so Father told me.'

My dad never spoke about the war. Yet four years later, you still felt it everywhere, every day, like a gritty layer of dust. You'd notice men who'd once been soldiers now begging on street corners, unable to work because of blindness, or burns, or missing arms or legs – and those were the injuries you *could* see. I'd overheard enough adults whispering to know that the war did funny things to people. We were lucky that all Dad had to show for it was a tremble in his hands. On the outside at least, he was all in one piece.

Gulping down the last of my breakfast, I wiped my fingers on my school skirt, then asked Mum again for the newspaper. I still wanted to read about the human feet.

Mum passed it to me. 'Quickly, then, or you'll be late.'

It didn't take long to read the story. As I'd suspected, it was a very odd turn of events.

3

The police, the report said, had been called to a central London address, where they found a man's feet on his hearth rug. The rest of him had vanished. His coat and hat were still hanging in their usual place in the hallway. Police named the man as Professor Selim Hanawati, a scholar of Middle Eastern art.

'Where's Professor Hanawati now?' I asked Mum. I didn't suppose he could've got far without his feet.

She gave me a narrow look. 'The poor man burned to death, Lilian. Every bit of him – apart from what they found. It's called *spontaneous human* ... something or other.'

Even with half a name, it didn't make much sense to me. People's bodies didn't burn by themselves.

Mum took the paper from me gently. 'You've frightened yourself now, haven't you?'

'No.' But it *had* stirred me up rather, and Mum, noticing this – as she always did – quickly homed in on another news story. 'Look, Lil! That archaeologist Howard Carter's gone back to Egypt to start digging again for Tutankhamun's tomb. One last go, apparently. Your grandad'll be interested, won't he?'

He wouldn't: Grandad had no time for Mr Carter. '*That* glory boy?' he'd called him. 'Without Lord

4

Carnarvon's money, he couldn't even afford the train ride to London!'

'Only because it's Egypt,' I said to Mum.

To say my grandad adored Egypt was an understatement. He'd named his Siamese cat Nefertiti after the queen. He'd travelled there, years ago, and been in love with the place ever since. It'd rubbed off on me, this fascination of his. Not that I'd a flying pig's chance of ever going there, but still.

As for the feet story, I couldn't shake it off. It stayed with me all day, through Latin, French, triple maths, and a science lesson about flammable liquids – bizarrely. To be blunt, school was a drag. I hated the place – or more precisely, St Kilda's College for Girls. Everyone was so proper, and so snooty with it. Yet listening to Mum and Dad you'd have thought our ship had well and truly come in when the scholarship offer arrived – *'Such an opportunity, Lilian!'* *'It's your chance for a brighter future!'* But believe me, life was much simpler when I went to the same school as the other kids on our street.

When I got home that night, the lights were off in our flat. The stove was cold. Dad was normally back before me, so it was a bit unusual. On the table, propped up against the salt pot, was a note from Mum.

We weren't a note-leaving type of family, so I knew straight away something had happened. And the jolt in my stomach told me the news was bad.

Skimming the message, I saw the words 'hospital' and 'Grandad', which troubled me even more. Only very sick people went to hospital. You had to pay for your treatment, and Grandad always said plenty of folks who went in never came out again.

Guessing poor Nefertiti would be worried too, I took the spare key to Grandad's from its hook. I didn't want to stay here on my own, imagining awful things. I'd go and feed his beloved cat, instead.

*

Grandad lived a few streets away above a shop that, according to the tatty sign over the door, sold 'Rarities and Antiquities' though I'd never seen him sell a single thing. Inside was a treasure trove of maps, vases, unpacked boxes and mouldy Turkish carpets stacked against the walls. He'd collected it all from his travels, though Mum reckoned it was mostly rubbish and he needed to get a cleaner in.

I covered the short distance to Grandad's at record pace. It was getting dark, the street lamps already lit, and the rain that'd dampened me on the way back from school had turned to sleet. For November, it was unusually cold.

Grandad's shop was shut up and dark. His rooms above it had their own entrance round the back, through a gate and down a side alley. As I lifted the gate latch, something warm rubbed against my legs, making me jump.

'Oh, cat!' I gasped out loud.

Nefertiti bounded ahead of me down the alley to wait on the back doorstep. It wasn't pitch dark here by any means: the streets all around were well lit. Yet a strange, shivery feeling came over me. I didn't want to go any further. And I certainly didn't want to go inside Grandad's flat.

Don't be stupid, I told myself. I'd only been here a few days ago for our usual Saturday afternoon tea. Yet even that, usually my favourite part of the week, had been a little bit odd.

We'd been drinking what Grandad called *chai* – dark, sugary tea in little glasses, Egyptian-style. It was a habit he'd picked up from his travels. Nefertiti, as usual, was draped like a fur stole around his shoulders. I'd never seen her sit like that on anyone else.

'Well, Lily,' Grandad announced, being the only person

not to call me plain old Lil. 'I've been thinking: I need to put my things in order, and I could do with your help.'

Now Grandad was often saying random things, which was one reason why I thought him so splendid. His cleverness didn't come from books or colleges but from going out into the world and getting grubby with it. You never knew quite what he'd come up with next.

On Saturday, though, he'd been coughing, enough for me to wonder if he wasn't well.

'What *things*?' I asked, though from the look on his face, it was obvious he wasn't talking about housework: he meant to write a will, and this alarmed me. 'You're not ill, are you?'

'Ill? Nah, tough as an old saddlebag, me.' Yet he quickly fell serious. 'It's a friend of mine from years back who's poorly. He wrote to me this week for the first time in years – troubled, he was, about something that happened between us a long time ago. We made a mistake, you see, and he's asking me to put it right.'

'So it's like his dying wish?' I said, because it sounded very mysterious.

'I sincerely hope not!' Grandad glared at me. 'He's sent me something to read – the writing's tiny and I can't find my blasted spectacles anywhere.'

Which wasn't surprising, given how untidy Grandad

8

was. But by now it was already five o'clock: time for me to go. We agreed I'd pop by another time to help him read it.

'Promise me you won't mention any of this to your mother,' Grandad said. 'You know how she's inclined to—'

'Fuss?' We both knew what Mum was like. I felt pleased to be trusted with something decent like a secret, when at home all I got to be responsible for were things like washing the supper dishes or making the beds. This was far more exciting. 'I'll not say a word to her, promise.'

'Or your father,' Grandad added.

I nodded. Not that I ever spoke to Dad about Grandad – the two of them hadn't shared a civil word in years. It was one of those family oddities you just knew, without being told exactly why.

Grandad tapped the side of his nose. 'Good girl, Lily. The nut doesn't reveal the tree it contains: it's an old Egyptian proverb, worth remembering.'

It was this I was thinking of now, as I stood at Grandad's door, telling myself not to be stupid. The only difference with his flat tonight was Grandad himself wasn't here. Yet the odd, chilly feeling wouldn't go away. It wasn't just me, either. The cat sensed it too. In one swift leap, Nefertiti was up on the neighbour's wall, fur on end.

'What's the matter, crosspatch?' I asked her.

She made a yowling noise that Grandad said was her way of talking. She wouldn't be coaxed down, not even with a square of chocolate I'd found in my coat pocket. So much for feeding her, when she wouldn't even come near me.

Even more bizarre was the key in the door. However much I twisted and jiggled it, the lock wouldn't open. I was in a right old fluster, and ready to give up and go home, when I saw a parcel. The postman had left it on the doorstep, behind the empty milk bottles. I bent down to pick it up. It was quite heavy, about the size of a shoebox, and wrapped in brown paper that was already wrinkled with damp. The name on the front was Grandad's: *Mr Ezra Wilkinson*. Ezra: a funny, old-fashioned name that Mum said was always given to the men in our family. My middle name – Ella – was as close to it as a girl's name could be.

Turning the parcel over to read the sender's name, I was in for a whopping great surprise.

Professor Selim Hanawati.

It was the man who'd died, who'd left behind his feet. And now it seemed he'd left something else, this time specifically for Grandad.

2

I headed straight home, clutching the parcel to my chest. Being back amongst the street lights, traffic, people going about their evening business, I hoped everything would seem a bit less weird: it didn't. I felt stunned. My brain, never good at staying quiet, leapt from one thing to the other as I walked.

My grandad in his younger days had travelled to Egypt, Turkey, Palestine, to buy copies of ancient relics to sell. Professor Hanawati was a Middle Eastern art expert. So did that mean this professor – this *dead* man – was the old friend Grandad had told me about, who'd got back in touch after all these years? He'd certainly never mentioned him before now. Nor had he ever talked about mistakes from the past.

I didn't want to dwell on strange coincidences. But it was hard not to, when the professor had died in such a peculiar way, and now Grandad was sick, all within the same twenty-four hours.

Back at ours, Mum still hadn't returned from the hospital. Dad was in the kitchen, arguing with the stove that wouldn't light: he didn't hear me come in. I went straight to my bedroom, which was really little more than a cupboard at the end of the hall. But it was mine, and it had a door on it that at times like this was good to shut behind you. Without taking off my coat, I sat on my bed to study the parcel closely. This was Grandad's package, not mine, I warned myself. But the urge to look inside was too strong.

I opened it.

Wrapped in the paper was a rough wooden box. It was about six inches tall and three inches deep, similar to the ones I'd seen Dad bring home at Christmas with a bottle of port inside. At the top was a lid, the clasp and hinges rusty, like it hadn't been opened for years. It opened now, though, smooth as anything – almost, rather creepily, as if it was willing me to look inside.

The box was full of musty-smelling straw. Digging my hand in, I could feel something cold and smooth. At first glance, it looked like a metal jar or vase of some sort. I took it out, holding it to the light. My breath caught. It was, without doubt, the most incredible thing I'd ever seen.

The jar had a stopper in its neck that wouldn't shift. It was fascinating, that stopper, shaped like an animal's head, with the long pointy snout and stand-up ears of Anubis, the Egyptian god who guided souls to the underworld. I recognised it from pictures Grandad had showed me, and our many visits to museums. The lid didn't want to come off, though. I tried pulling it, turning it. I even held the whole jar upside down and gave it a little shake. There were no signs that it was meant to open: no latch or clasp, yet it sounded hollow, and though I might've been imagining it, when I shook it, something moved inside.

Now, I'd been in Grandad's shop enough to know a nice piece when I saw one, but this jar was seriously old-looking – and the things Grandad collected generally weren't. They were fakes – copies of lovely old things at affordable prices. You could buy them in the street in Egypt, apparently.

This jar was in a whole different league. It was covered all over in little pictures of animals and birds and squiggly lines: hieroglyphics. Though the jar was grimy with dirt, you could see it was made out of gold. To be honest, it was so beautiful, it made me a bit afraid. The only place I'd ever seen things half as magnificent was in cabinets at the British Museum. I couldn't think why my grandad had been sent something quite so extraordinary.

Question after question bubbled up in my head, and there was no Grandad there to answer them, which was mightily frustrating. The only thing for it was to go and see him. Not to take him flowers or grapes or whatever people did when they visited hospitals, but to give him the parcel. He'd know what to do with it. What it was all about. I only hoped he wasn't too horribly ill to see me.

Out in the hallway, the front door slammed. Wet things were being hung up, the rattle of an umbrella returned to its stand: signs that Mum was home. My heart thumped uncomfortably as I heard her say something to Dad in a low voice. Then she called to me: 'Lil? You there?'

'Coming!' I answered.

Tucking the jar back inside the box, I hid it under my covers and, though I was dreading it, went to hear the news from the hospital.

*

What Mum told me was worrying to say the least: Grandad had a consumption in his lungs. He had a fever, too, and other strange symptoms that the doctors thought were malaria.

'*Malaria?*' I didn't understand. How could you get malaria in North London?

'He got it years ago on his travels. A flare-up of an old illness, the doctor said – and what with his lungs …' Mum started to cry. Quietly. Miserably.

It made me teary too. I hated it when she got upset. Mostly, it was over much smaller things than this, the stuff a smile or a pat on the arm would make better. But this was serious, and called for tea. I gave Mum hers with extra sugar, which usually did the trick when she was low.

'How will he ever pay for the hospital?' Mum sighed, teacup in hand.

Dad stared broodily at the fire. 'We can hardly manage our own bills, love. Don't ask me to start helping your father now.'

Revived a bit, Mum then started fretting over me: 'You're not to visit him, Lil, I'm warning you, he's infectious.' And Dad chipped in with: 'She'll be at school, not hanging around hospital wards.'

So I nodded and tried to look sensible, though my mind was already made up: I *was* going to see him tomorrow, and they couldn't stop me. I stayed tight-lipped about the strange business with the parcel too.

Mum already had enough to worry about, and Dad, a stickler for doing things properly, would probably make me take it to the police.

*

That night I couldn't sleep for toffee. Worrying about Grandad was bad enough, but I'd not counted on the jar disturbing me like it did. I'd left the box on my chair, but every time I nearly nodded off, my eyes would ping open and I'd find myself staring at it again. Eventually, I put the light on. Then my mind started playing tricks: was the parcel moving? What was that rustling sound? Was the package *unwrapping* itself?

It was stupid, thinking like this. But in the end I only felt better once the parcel was out of sight under my bed. My room became familiar again too: the chair heaped with clothes, a rag rug on the bare floor, thin curtains at the window that always let in a draught.

'We could make it look nicer, couldn't we, eh?' Mum said when we first came to live here. 'A bit of lace, a few dried flowers?'

I'd pulled a face and she sighed. 'Oh, Lil! You're so plain and practical. Sometimes I think you'd rather have been born a boy!'

Actually, she had a point. Yet as soon as she'd said it, she kissed the top of my head and insisted she didn't mean it.

Even now the only decoration was on the wall above my bed, where I'd stuck a postcard Grandad bought me on our last visit to the British Museum. It was of the Rosetta Stone, that big grey slab covered in ancient writing that meant the rest of the world could translate hieroglyphics.

Turning out my bedside lamp, I hoped I'd finally go to sleep. But instead, the darkness swirled with ancient symbols. When I tried to think of something else, I kept coming back to Egypt, only this time it was today's other news story, the one about Howard Carter and Tutankhamun's tomb.

Despite what Grandad thought of Mr Carter, people *were* fascinated by the story. There was something about it – a brave explorer searching for unknown treasures – that captured the imagination like a good old-fashioned adventure tale, the sort Dad would've read as a boy. I devoured them myself too sometimes, when my Latin homework got too dull.

For years archaeologists had been digging in the place they called the Valley of the Kings. They'd discovered plenty of royal tombs – those of Thutmose and Rameses II being two of the famous ones – yet no one had ever found the pharaoh Tutankhamun. They'd given up looking, all except for one man: Howard Carter. Obsessed with the missing tomb, he was back in Egypt for one last search.

Dad said the story captured people's hearts because Tutankhamun had died young, which made us think of all our soldiers whose war graves were also lost. But I reckoned it had just as much to do with treasure, because we knew how the Egyptians buried their kings with loads of gold. It was a hopeful story too, in a way that the other one about human feet definitely wasn't.

The worst news of all, though, was Grandad's. The business with his lungs I'd perhaps seen coming, but *malaria*? I didn't know you could get that again once you'd had it. Funny how something from all those years ago had come back to make trouble now.

3

'You can't come in. It's rest time,' said the nurse at
Brompton Hospital the next morning. 'Visiting hours
start at two.'

I looked at my watch: four hours to go. It'd taken
a fair bit of daring to get here, when I should've been
in class at St Kilda's doing a spelling test: Dad had
wished me luck for it as he was leaving for work. I wasn't
looking forward to lying to him later, when he'd ask
me how it went.

'I have to speak to Mr Ezra Wilkinson.' I said again.
'He's my grandad.'

The nurse folded her arms. 'He didn't teach you
any manners, did he?'

People from round our way weren't full of airs and
graces, it was true. But I could see I was going to have
to try harder. 'Please, it's very urgent.'

'So urgent it can't wait till this afternoon?' she asked.

To be truthful, I didn't want to come back here

again. The hospital smelled horrible, of carbolic mixed with old vegetables. It made me feel ill, which was odd for a place meant to make people better.

'Please,' I begged. 'I'll be quick.'

Over her shoulder I glimpsed rows of snowy-white beds; knowing Grandad was in one of them, just feet away, was infuriating. It crossed my mind to dodge past the nurse.

Then I caught her taking in my St Kilda's blazer – horrid bright red – that showed at the wrists of my coat. And the ugly felt hat on my head and my satchel, strapped across me, all of which bore the school crest. I might as well have worn a sign around my neck.

'Shouldn't you be in school?' the nurse asked. 'Perhaps I should give them a telephone call.'

'I'm going, don't worry,' I muttered, and hurried back down the stairs.

*

Out in the street, I kicked myself. I should've known there'd be visiting hours at the hospital. Not only that, skipping school was risky: there was always someone, somewhere, waiting to peach on you. In adventure stories the heroes have a bunch of like-minded pals on hand to help. It was different trying to be brave by yourself.

Most of my old friends had been boys – Neddy, Joe, Brian and Bobby Fitzpatrick. When we weren't at school, we'd play Crab Apple Cricket or Bulldog out in the street.

Then I'd got the scholarship to St Kilda's.

'Can you smell brains?' Bobby asked the others, on the first day of term, when they'd gone down the street to their new school and I'd gone up it to mine. They didn't speak to me after that.

The girls at St Kilda's were even harder to be pally with. Some days, when no one was looking, I'd get a bit upset. And I felt bad for that too, because it wasn't like I had something proper to be sad about, like a dad or a brother dead in the war.

At some point, I realised I was lost. This was a part of South London I'd never been to before. The road was busy with shoppers and nannies pushing babies in prams. Weaving in amongst traffic, the newspaper boys shouted the day's headlines – about King George, our new prime minister Mr Bonar Law, and Ireland now a country of its own. And – my ears pricked – Egypt:

'Courageous Howard Carter just days from finding

missing boy king! Experts convinced he'll discover a tomb full of gold!'

I hugged the satchel tight against my hip. Inside it, in a box, was another piece of gold, a jar so unsettling that last night I'd had to hide it. Even in broad daylight, I'd not completely shaken off that feeling of dread. It didn't help that I knew next to nothing about this extraordinary find.

Enough misery-mongering.

It was hours till visiting hours started, and I was on the wrong side of London to go to school. With time to kill, I decided to do some digging of my own.

*

The bus ride to the British Museum cost me my last thruppence. On arrival, I went straight upstairs. The Egyptian exhibits weren't in one big room, but a series of little ones that ran into each other. To my mind, it was the best bit of the whole museum. I loved the old dark wood cabinets and the way the floor dipped and creaked when you walked. The blinds, always down at the windows, made a sort of all-day twilight. There were vases, statues called *shabtis* for guarding dead bodies, swords, beads, even mummified pets.

Everywhere you looked something fascinating glinted back at you – like in Grandad's shop, only older and more beautiful.

The Egyptian rooms were usually very quiet. So I'd not expected to find anyone else up there, let alone two children sitting cross-legged on the floor of the very first room.

It pulled me up short. 'Oh!'

The girl, who was drawing, glanced up from her notepad. Sat beside her was a boy, also drawing, who carried on doing so until she nudged him.

'Hey!' he yelped, as his pencil jerked across the paper.

'I thought you said no one came here,' the girl complained.

I was thinking the same, embarrassed and a bit annoyed. It was then I noticed the girl's pinafore – red, like mine, with the yellow school badge on the bib. She wasn't hiding hers under a coat, either, but wearing it for all to see.

'You at St Kilda's, then?' I asked. It came out a bit abruptly, though I hadn't meant it to. My run-in with the nurse had left me still feeling a bit spiky.

The girl tugged at her dress. 'I'd hardly wear *this* out of choice. And as for that *poisonous* school hat!'

She then saw mine, still rammed on to my head.

I snatched it off quick: how I hated the stupid thing. The girl thought this funny and laughed. I wasn't sure if I was meant to join in, but she had such a cheeky lopsided grin that I found myself grinning back. No one I knew smiled like that, or if they did I'd not seen them do it for a very long time.

'You hate St Kilda's too?' she asked.

'The students are a bit snooty,' I admitted.

The girl pulled a face. 'Millicent Thorpe and pals, d'you mean?'

I nodded. They were the snobbiest of the lot.

I'd never seen this girl at St Kilda's, though, and she had the sort of face you'd remember – brown-skinned, green-eyed, freckled. Her hair was jet black and sprang out in perfect corkscrew curls. Instead of rushing off, I set down my satchel next to their bags, coats, mittens, hats and scarves, which they'd dumped in a heap inside the door.

'I'm Tulip.' The girl was still smiling.

Tulip: it sounded *daring*, like a dancer or a flapper girl's name. She had that look to her too – tall and slender.

'I'm Lil, short for Lilian,' I replied, thinking how dull my name was in comparison.

'That's Oz, my brother.' Tulip meant the boy. 'He

doesn't say much, so don't think him rude. He loves this museum. We come here all the time.'

The boy was about ten, I'd say, and looked just like her. He wasn't wearing a uniform at all, which made me think he didn't go to school, the lucky so and so. I felt a pang of envy for him and his sister, who seemed quite happy in each other's company. Times like these I wished I had a bigger family of my own.

'He's good at drawing,' I remarked.

He'd almost filled a fresh page with hieroglyphics that he was copying from a coffin in the centre of the room. Some of the images – the snake, falcon and ankh – were also on Grandad's jar, which got me interested.

'Does he know what they mean?' I asked Tulip.

'He's learning,' she replied. 'Why, do you understand them?'

'Only a bit.' I pointed to some of the rougher sketches on Oz's paper. 'That dog creature? It's Anubis, god of the underworld. And this one, with the open wings – it's Isis, goddess of protection.'

Both were on the jar.

Thinking I might be on to something, I moved closer to the coffin for a better look. I'd been in this room loads of times before, but I'd never noticed the name on the display card inside the cabinet. Yet there it was, in black and white:

Item 475: Coffin of unknown nobleman,
decorated in relief-work typical of
the Upper Nile. Thought to date back
to 1350 BC.
    Professor Selim Hanawati, Luxor,
Egypt. May 1900.

I whistled under my breath, not quite believing my luck. The first place I'd looked and here it was, a whopping great clue! The coffin, with its connection to Professor Hanawati, might well have come from the same part of Egypt as the jar. Perhaps he'd found it on the same trip.

But I reminded myself that Anubis and Isis were often found on goods buried in ancient Egyptian graves, and I should probably calm down. Yes, it was likely the jar *was* something to do with death, but that didn't mean this coffin here belonged to the same dead person.

'It's only a nobleman's coffin.' Oz spoke behind me, making me jump. 'If he'd been a pharaoh, the whole lot would've been gold.'

'I suppose so,' I agreed.

'Most of the tombs they've found so far have been "robbed in antiquity",' Oz went on. 'So even if Howard Carter does find Tutankhamun, chances are a thief will have got there first.'

I looked at him sideways: for someone who didn't talk much, he had a fair bit to say about Egyptian burials.

'My brother Alex taught me about Egypt. He was an expert,' Oz explained proudly.

Tulip rolled her eyes: 'Oh, Oz, don't go on about Alex. I'm sure Lil doesn't want to hear our whole family history.'

Actually, I was wondering what Oz, or this brother of his, would make of Grandad's jar, when a woman rushed into the room. 'I should have realised you'd both be up here!'

Tulip looked so horrified that for a moment I panicked: was the woman one of those school attendance officers who made trouble if they caught you skiving?

Then Tulip said, 'Oh lordy, Mama! I'm sorry! I forgot the time!'

This was her *mother*?

She didn't look like Oz or Tulip – she was white, and yet her children both had brown skin. Her clothes were the sort *my* mother wouldn't be seen dead in – an orange dress, purple stockings and the brightest red lipstick. Now, I wasn't one to get excited about dresses and stuff, but even I could see that this woman was terrifically glamorous. And how amazing that she didn't bat an eyelash at the fact Tulip wasn't in school!

'Hurry up, darlings,' the woman drawled in an accent that wasn't English. 'Mr Pemberton's joining us for lunch.'

'Clever you!' Tulip started rooting through the pile by the door, grabbing her scarf and bag. Oz packed away his sketchbook. A flurry of putting on coats and hats followed.

'Goodbye, Lil!' Tulip waved. Then all three of them were gone. The room was suddenly quiet and rather empty. It was odd to miss people I'd only just met, but that's how it felt.

It was early still – by my watch, just past midday – but with no more money for a bus fare, I decided to start the long walk back to Brompton Hospital. I went to pick up my satchel from where I'd left it by the door, but it wasn't there. Someone must've moved it.

Panicky minutes followed as I searched the room. Then, thank crikey, I found it, wedged between the open door and the wall. Except, when I pulled it free and lifted the flap to check everything was still inside, I realised *this* satchel wasn't mine. Yes, it was conker-brown leather, with two front buckles and the St Kilda's crest on the front. But inside was a sketchbook and pencils, and the name 'Tulip Mendoza' with an address in Highgate written underneath.

The daft girl had taken the wrong bag. With the jar still inside.

By the time I'd raced outside, the Mendozas had well and truly gone. I couldn't believe I'd been so careless. There was nothing I could do about it, though, apart from not tell Grandad I'd lost it. At least I knew where Tulip lived. And I had to admit I rather liked having an excuse to see her and her brother again.

4

When I arrived at the hospital, Grandad was asleep. He was at the far end of the ward – 'in a nice quiet spot,' said a different nurse to this morning's, thankfully, with a lovely, soft-as-feathers voice. I'd hoped to find him propped up in bed, glad to see me, but as I passed the other patients my heart sank: no one here looked well enough for visitors.

Behind Grandad's bed, the windows were open. The fresh air made it so bitterly cold the bed was heaped with blankets: all I could see was a tuft of his steel-grey hair sticking out from underneath.

I pulled up a chair.

'That you, Lily?' he said without looking.

'How did you guess?'

'You smell of rain,' he replied. 'Your mother would've had the good sense to bring her umbrella.'

The blankets twitched. Grandad's face appeared. I wasn't ready for the shock. It was only a few days since

I'd last seen him, but he'd got so much thinner, like his skin had shrunk down to his bones.

'How's my cat? You been feeding her?' he croaked.

'I've been trying,' I admitted. 'Don't tell Mum but I skived off school to come and see you.'

His attempt at laughing turned into a horrible cough. Mum had worried about him passing on the infection, but what bothered me far more was how sick he looked.

'Listen, I've something to tell you.' I dropped my voice to a nervous whisper. 'A parcel turned up at your shop. It's from a man called Professor Hanawati, and inside it is the most wonderful—'

'He sent the *jar*?' Grandad interrupted. He tried – and failed – to sit up.

I nodded. It was becoming painfully obvious how important this jar was. And how stupid I'd been to let it out of my sight.

'Why did the professor send it to you?' I asked. 'It looks like it belongs in a museum.'

Grandad spluttered. 'A *museum*? That's how all this terrible business started!'

'What terrible business?'

'The curse,' he whispered.

He looked sicker than ever, suddenly. Sweat rolled off his face, pooling in his collarbones and soaking the pillow and blankets. It was horrible to see him like this.

'It's an unusual jar, that's all. I'm sure it's not cursed,' I said, trying to reassure him.

He grabbed my arm. 'I mean it, Lily. There's a curse on that jar. It took Hanawati twenty years to realise.'

Perhaps it was only the fever talking, but I admit I began to feel unsettled. The professor's death was very strange, and the jar had certainly unnerved me.

'If I don't recover,' Grandad croaked. 'If the curse is on me now—'

'Sssh! Don't say that!' I broke in, though it was dawning on me that he might be talking sense. Since that letter had come from the professor, he'd got sicker and sicker, and now the jar had been passed on to him . . .

I grew suddenly afraid.

'What do you want me to do?' I asked. 'If this is a curse, what will break it?'

'Send the jar back, Lily!' Grandad gasped.

'To Egypt?'

He nodded desperately. 'To the hotel . . . Mr Ibrahim . . . before the curse . . .'

I sat back in my seat, stumped already. How on earth was I going to get a jar back to Egypt?

'Which hotel?' I pressed him. 'And who's Mr Ibrahim?'

'Winter ... palace ... reception ...' he wheezed.

'Winter Palace? Is that the hotel's name?'

He coughed. I tried to help him with a drink, but he pushed the cup away, sloshing water all over the bed.

'You have to ... otherwise ... too late ...' Another coughing fit seized him. It was a horrible, bed-shaking, scouring noise that went on and on until the nurse came running with a bowl. I didn't see what Grandad spat into it, but it sounded wet and solid. When he wiped his mouth afterwards there was blood on the cloth.

It was awful to see him so unwell.

The nice nurse, seeing my shock, nudged me from my seat. 'You'd better go, love.'

But Grandad was beckoning me to come closer. 'I shouldn't have taken it. Not mine to decide ... all those years ago ...'

'He's rambling,' the nurse insisted. 'Really, you should go.'

'He wants me to help him,' I said desperately. 'I don't know what to do.'

'Give the poor chap a bit of peace and quiet, that's what he needs,' she replied.

When Grandad tried to speak, he really couldn't breathe. The nurse propelled me away from the bed with her free hand, as with the other she thrust the bowl back under Grandad's chin.

'Believe me, it's better if you don't see him like this,' she said.

It was too late for that. I don't think I'd ever witnessed another living person in such a dreadful state, never mind someone this dear to me. It was like being thumped right in the heart.

Knowing how much Grandad would hate me to cry, I held on to my tears until I got outside. Even then it was awkward to be sobbing in public, with people staring and hurrying past as if my sadness was catching. Returning the jar to Egypt wasn't going to be easy. But Grandad had asked me to, so I'd do it. First, though, I had to get it back from Tulip. It was too late – and too far – to go to Highgate today. It would have to be tomorrow, after school, if Tulip didn't turn up at St Kilda's. I wasn't expecting her to, somehow.

Then there was Professor Hanawati's letter to Grandad, which might tell me something about the Egyptian hotel and, I thought with a shudder, the curse. How strange that only days ago I'd mentioned dying wishes, and now here we were – one man dead, another dangerously ill – and what mattered most was a jar being returned to its rightful place.

On the long walk home I caught myself remembering something from a couple of years ago. Dad had taken us to a funeral: a big one – a *procession*, he'd called it. Mum had brushed off our best coats and, as it was a Thursday, I was allowed to skip school to attend. Crowds were expected all along the route from Victoria station to Westminster Abbey where the coffin would be buried like a king's. Not that we knew who the dead person was, but that, said Dad, was exactly the point.

The Unknown Warrior was what they called him. Dad explained how, in the battlefields of France, they'd dug up four unmarked bodies and chosen one at random. That body could've been a private, a lieutenant, a captain – *anyone*. He represented all the men of all ranks, all ages, who'd died in the war. Put like that, it sounded grand and honourable.

Yet all week in the playground – I was still at my local junior school back then – we'd been gossiping about what would be inside the coffin. Neddy reckoned it was full of jumbled-up body parts because that was all they could find. Someone else – Bobby, I think – said it was actually a dead dog. But Rita Farley, one of the older girls, said she knew for a fact the coffin would be open, so we'd get to see for ourselves. I was horrified and fascinated by this idea.

Mum had invited Grandad to come with us to the funeral. The plan was to meet him outside Woolworths. From there we'd catch the bus to Green Park, then walk to Constitution Hill, which was one of those wide city roads where the procession was due to pass.

On the morning itself, we waited ten, maybe twenty minutes for Grandad to arrive, me done up in my best frock with a stupid bow in my hair, fidgeting with excitement. Mum kept glancing at Dad, who was starting to get annoyed. When our bus pulled up there was still no sign of Grandad. Dad said he wasn't waiting any longer, which meant we weren't, either.

Boarding the bus, I was very close to tears. I didn't understand why a funeral for someone we didn't know was more important than waiting for someone we did. Even when the funeral was over, and I'd seen the black shiny horses pulling the gun carriage and the coffin draped with the Union flag, which wasn't open at all, I still felt disappointed. All we saw of the Unknown Soldier was a dented tin helmet. And even that wasn't his, so Dad said.

Afterwards, Grandad didn't apologise or explain why he'd not come along that day. In fact, it was never mentioned again.

Thinking of it now, the whole process – the dead bodies, the long journey from France, the public funeral – reminded me of the bizarre situation I was in. Maybe back then it'd reminded Grandad too, of what he and the professor had taken. In the end, the Unknown Soldier was laid to rest in his home country, but the jar was still thousands of miles from Egypt – actually, in Highgate, to be precise, at the house of someone I'd only just met.

5

That night at the supper table, I told a lie.

'Easier than the last one,' I said, when Dad asked how the spelling test had gone today at school.

He'd caught me off guard. I was so busy thinking about hotels and Professor Hanawati, I'd forgotten the day I should've had.

'Go on, then, tell me, what was the hardest word in the test?' Dad asked.

I said the first thing that came into my head: 'Reincarnation.'

'Did you get full marks?'

'Umm . . . no.'

'Which words did you get wrong? Because they're the ones you ought to be practising, you know.' It was typical Dad, wanting me to be cleverer, faster, better, and I did try, but tonight it was exhausting. I got up from the table and started clearing the dishes.

'Lilian,' he said sharply. 'I'm talking to you.'

'Oh, leave her be. She's worried about her grandad,' Mum chided.

I was, in ways they couldn't imagine.

'Well, she'd better not be slipping behind. I'll be on to her teachers if she is.' Dad shook out the paper.

Once he'd disappeared behind it, Mum leaned towards me, whispering: '*I'm* proud of you, Lil. You've got your grandad's spirit – far more than I ever did. There's more to the world than spelling tests, he'd say – and he's right.'

Dear Mum: she was trying to be kind, but it felt like a nudge in the ribs, reminding me of my promise to Grandad. I smiled stiffly; I couldn't tell her about the jar or the curse, could I? I wasn't even meant to have gone to the hospital in the first place.

Times like this I wondered what it would be like to have someone my age to talk to – to share private, secret stuff that wasn't for grown-ups' ears. Like Tulip did, I bet, with her two brothers, the lucky devil.

After supper was cleared and a pot of tea made, Mum and Dad settled by the stove. Every evening it was the same. We'd sit quietly, rarely speaking, though often I'd glance up and notice how sad they looked. Dad, I supposed, might be thinking about the war. As for Mum, I didn't know. Sometimes she'd have tears in

39

her eyes. Other times, she'd rest a hand on her stomach and sigh.

Tonight, though, I couldn't sit quietly, not with Professor Hanawati's letter at Grandad's, just waiting to be read.

'Has Nefertiti been fed yet?' I asked. 'I'll go if you like.'

I knew full well how hard it was to coax my parents out of their chairs once they'd settled down. And it was just the sort of little job they'd count on me to do.

'Good girl,' Mum said. 'Don't be long.'

*

A short time later, I was heading down Grandad's side alley. This time I'd brought a torch, but still felt wary as I turned the corner. On the doorstep were two bottles of milk and one of cream, and Nefertiti crouched between them. The second she saw me, she stood up purring.

'Glad to see you're happier tonight, miss,' I said, crouching down to scratch her chin. She was probably hungry, I supposed.

But when the door unlocked easily enough, I began

to wonder if something was already shifting. Now I knew about the curse, and what I had to do to break it, maybe it was a sign I was on the right track.

It felt odd to go inside with no Grandad there to greet me. The hallway was so familiar: the crooked lampshade he'd never bothered to straighten, the coat stand, the stairs, the passageway leading to the shop. It made me come over all upset.

Though being in the shop itself felt better – a comfort, even. The room was so full of Grandad, it was like he was here with me. The shelves on every wall were crammed with books, plates, carvings, more boxes. Even the alarming bits – the strange face masks, the stuffed animals with glass-bead eyes – were all reasons why I loved coming to visit.

In the bay window was Grandad's desk, messy as ever. I flicked through coal bills, newspaper clippings – a fair few of which, I noticed, were to do with Egypt and, more specifically, Mr Carter.

Moving a heap of notebooks aside, I found a half-eaten corned-beef sandwich. A quick sniff confirmed it'd been there for some time – longer than Grandad had been sick. He was like me where food was concerned: it'd take something really shocking to put him off what he was eating.

What looked to be Dr Hanawati's letter was underneath the sandwich. It wasn't a short one, either, but a good five or six pages long, and covered in stale breadcrumbs. The paper was tissue-thin, and a lovely, unusual blue colour. I scanned it for a signature, which – oddly – was at the bottom of the very first page. Like most people's it was a squiggle, but I was able to recognise the 'H' at the start of the name and the 'ti' at the end, to know this was what I was looking for.

I sat down in the nearest chair. It felt strange to be about to read a dead man's letter. A bit eerie. A bit sad. But, I was intrigued to hear what he had to say.

Dear Ezra, it began,

You will know how hard it is for me to admit to being wrong, but I must tell you, your instincts regarding the Egyptian canopic jar were right all along: it does, I fear, carry a terrible curse. We should have left it in Egypt where it belongs. The death of a young boy just days after he discovered it in that queer little rock-face tomb was no accident. Nor should we have argued and fought over the jar. We were good chums, Ezra, but we let the jar breed bad feeling between us. It poisoned our friendship,

I'm sad to say.

Many years ago you told me never to darken your door again, and I respected your wish. Now I find I must communicate with you. I have important, terrible news. Neither of us knew there was anything inside the jar, did we? Yet recently I've discovered it holds a secret.

Let me explain. For years the jar stayed packed away in my attic, all but forgotten. Last month, something changed. For some unknown reason, the jar began to play on my mind, and when I retrieved it from the attic, I heard a rattling sound, indicating an object was inside. It struck me as strange that neither you nor I had heard such a sound when we brought the jar home all that time ago, in such unhappy circumstances.

On removing the lid – which took considerable effort – I found a papyrus scroll, rolled up tightly, folded and tied with a leather thong. There was also something stuffed into the base of the jar – a scrap of old linen, probably – that I couldn't dislodge.

It was the scroll that captivated my interest, and so I set about trying to translate it. The writing was hard to decipher. It wasn't the hieroglyphs I would have expected to see on an important document, but the informal demotic Egyptian of a personal account. I spent hours – days! – at my desk, poring over this discovery. As finds go it was almost as exciting as our first sighting of the jar itself – remember that, Ezra? How we swooned when we saw it on that market stall! We could not believe Mr Carter had dismissed it as an 'insignificant' piece. How stupid he would feel now if he could read this translation. When you see whose name appears at the very start of the account, you will understand my elation.

Yet I have to warn you, my excitement was short-lived. On commencing the translation, I was overcome with a terrible feeling of dread; I can't describe it more eloquently than that. These past couple of weeks I've suffered nightmares, headaches, fevers. The doctor says it is nervous exhaustion but I know it is something more sinister, Ezra, something linked to the jar. Of course, no one believes me. My own dear wife looks at me across the dinner table each night as if I were insane. I assure you, I am not.

The jar is back in its box. I cannot bear to look at it or even have it in my study with me any more. Every day I live in fear of some nameless terror. The curse is upon me. Much more of this and I will *have to rid myself of the jar, for my safety and well-being. Perhaps I might return it to you, who always understood its power better than me?*

Meanwhile, I send you what of the scroll I have translated so far: there is more to come but my progress is proving slower with what remains. You will be interested to read it, I know, and can, I hope, be of help.

Your old friend,
Selim Hanawati

I sat with my head in my hands. The letter was a lot to digest. How uncanny that Professor Hanawati had guessed something awful was going to happen to him. It made me more scared for Grandad, too, because the letter confirmed that the curse really did exist. So why, after all these years, had it started up again? And what was wrapped in linen, in the bottom of the jar? There was no mention of the hotel Grandad spoke about, either.

The remaining sheets of paper in my hand were the translation, I guessed. Grandad was right, the writing was tiny and cramped, so much so I had to move closer to the lamp to read it properly.

Thebes, Ancient Egypt

I, Lysandra, have been trusted to scribe the final days
of our king, Tutankhamun. Be warned, this is not
the official account: mine is about the boy who didn't
want to be pharaoh, who was at his happiest pelting
my brother with pomegranates.

I stopped. Read the first lines again.

This was about Tutankhamun? *The* Tutankhamun,
who Howard Carter was so desperate to find, whose
name was in the news almost every day now?

Just in case I'd got it wrong, I held the paper directly
underneath the light. No, the name was there, all right.
Though I couldn't believe what I was reading . . .

There's a saying amongst our people: 'Let your face
shine,' because no one wants to live an unhappy life
here on earth, and then be stuck with it forever in
the afterlife. So when I see Kyky limping towards our
house with a face like an old goat's, I sense trouble is
on the way.

'Shall I call Maya?' I ask him.

Maya is my older brother and Kyky's dearest

friend. Only a short stretch of courtyard separates our house from the steps to the royal palace where Kyky lives. That's not his proper name: Maya made it up when he was little. He's been Kyky to our family ever since.

My brother is taller than any of us nowadays. He has long legs as thin as a stork's but is strong and healthy and happy: all the things Kyky isn't. But Kyky is also King Tutankhamun of Egypt. Often, I think he hates this role. It weighs him down, bores him. He'd rather idle his days away with Maya, climbing trees, hunting rodents. Neither has yet seen seventeen summers – they are still young and prone to silliness. Our mother pretends not to see it but I know she doesn't approve. She sews and tuts, sews and tuts, which will be her lot for eternity if she's not careful.

Kyky leans on his walking stick, a little out of breath. 'Call him in a moment, Lysandra,' he replies. 'First, I need to talk to you.'

This takes me by surprise. When people visit me, they come to share their dreams. My grandfather was the first in our family with a gift for dream reading. Now the honour has been passed to me. A person's dreams tell you their hopes and fears, the road they

47

will follow into the afterlife. The skill is to listen. To hold each part of what they say in your hands.

'A dream is like a melon,' I tell people. 'It's not until you cut open the skin that you find the sweet truth inside.'

As I'm only young – four summers behind my brother – I'm still learning the skill. I'm quieter than him too – a watcher, my mother calls me. She says it's why the gift came to me.

Today, Kyky looks pale. I hope we're not in for another bout of illness. The fever leaves him weaker every time, and I know I'm not alone in noticing it. There are those at the palace who watch Kyky – every limp, every sweat, every meal left untouched. No one watches more than his godfather, Ay, whom Kyky leans on like a son to a wise father. He does little without Ay's approval, and in my view, spends far too much time seeking it. I don't trust Ay. He has the eyes of a hungry wolf watching a weakening lamb.

'Come inside,' I say to Kyky.

There's no sun; the wind off the river is too brisk for sitting outside. So Kyky follows me in to where the stove is hot because my mother is baking. She sees us coming, bows and scuttles off, tucking the basket of already-baked bread under her arm.

'Please, sit,' I say, gesturing to the cushions on the floor.

Kyky shakes his head. He's glancing nervously towards the doorway, expecting Maya to appear.

I don't sit either. 'Bad dreams?'

'Terrible dreams!' he hisses. 'For the last few nights it's been the same. I'm chasing someone and though I run and run, I can't reach them.'

There's a fresh insect bite on his left cheek. He should have a net covering his bed. I wonder why his servant whose job it is to tend to these things isn't being more careful. The fevers that come with such a bite are dangerous. So too are the coughs that plague him every winter.

'Are you sick?' I ask, because this sounds like a fever dream. I hear plenty of them and they usually mean very little.

'No, Lysandra. For once I'm not.'

I'm more interested now. 'And how does it end, this dream of yours?'

'I reach a dead end – a wall, a locked door, a ravine – it changes every time.' He shivers slightly. 'Behind me, I hear animals growling. Scorpions run across my feet.'

I mull over what he's told me, a coldness in my veins; I need to hear more of this dream.

'The person you're chasing – do you see them?' I ask.

'I don't get a good look – oh!' He stops, startled, as Maya strides into the room.

My brother, wrapped in a blanket against the chill, looks more bony-limbed than ever.

'Not trying to charm my sister, are you?' he asks, giving Kyky a playful nudge.

He's being ridiculous: Kyky has a wife – Queen Ankhesenamun – chosen for him by the men of his inner circle. She's very beautiful, with amber eyes and trailing black hair, though she's almost as old as our mother – which, people say, is why her babies don't tend to live.

'Go and jump in the river,' I tell Maya, scowling.

My brother grins: 'That's an idea! Coming, Kyky?'

Once they've gone to get up to whatever mischief takes their fancy, I let out the long, worried breath I've been holding in. This dream of Kyky's troubles me.

The sun stays hidden for days on end. Everything is cold – the ground we walk on, the water we bathe in, the linen we wear. Kyky's father was a wayward pharaoh who had favourites among the gods. It brought chaos to our country and people are saying the god Amun is still offended, which is why the sun refuses to shine.

'I've never known a winter so miserable or so dark,' Mother says. She keeps our oil lamps lit all day so she can see well enough to sew.

I'm struggling to concentrate on my scribing work. All morning I make mistakes on the papyrus. Mother scolds me: 'Whatever's the matter, Lysandra? Come, sit closer to the light.'

But my mind keeps wandering back to Kyky's dream. A dead end means something – or someone – is blocking his journey through this life and on to the next. It's a bad omen. So too are the scorpions, which conjure up all things poisonous. I can't explain to Mother that the darkness isn't in the room but in my head.

We're saved by Maya, who rushes in from outside, bringing the cold air with him.

'I have news!' he says. 'The king's decided to hold a feast day for Amun tomorrow, to win back his favour!'

'Ay has decided it, you mean,' I mutter. Yet despite my mood, I'm glad. I've missed the sun.

'What can we do to help?' Mother asks, ever practical.

'Your flatbread, Mother. Kyky is requesting it.' Maya turns to me. 'You can help Roti with the horses. There's going to be chariot racing. For once Kyky's dear godfather is letting him have his way.'

Chariot racing is one of Kyky's favourite sports. It's also dangerous, noisy, smelly and both thrilling and terrifying to watch.

'He's not taking part, is he?' I ask. The thought makes me anxious.

Maya laughs. 'Don't look so worried! It's a feast day, not a funeral.'

I pray my joyful brother is right.

PART TWO

It was for us to prove we were worthy of the trust.

HOWARD CARTER, ARCHAEOLOGIST

6

'How long does it take to feed a cat?' Dad quizzed me when I got home.

I didn't have an answer ready this time, either. As I took my coat off and warmed my hands by the stove, I was still in a daze. Though I'd expected the jar to be from Egypt nothing had prepared me for Lysandra's story, which connected it to the most famous pharaoh in the whole world. I kept thinking about Kyky, the boy who'd wanted a normal life, and who sounded nothing like the treasure-laden king Howard Carter was chasing after.

And that wasn't all. Professor Hanawati had been working on the rest of the translation when he died. In his letter, he'd promised 'more to come'. Just the part I'd read threw up questions enough:

Was the 'little rock-face tomb' Professor Hanawati mentioned the same one Mr Carter was searching for? Was the site where archaeologists and news reporters from across the world were gathering really the right place? It didn't sound that peaceful to me.

Which brought me back to the curse.

Howard Carter was the reason the curse was active again. He had to be. The news of his final search in the Valley of the Kings had broken just before Professor Hanawati's letter arrived at Grandad's. In digging for the tomb, Mr Carter had stirred up the past.

Saying I had a headache, I went early to bed, where I read Lysandra's account all over again. This time, I noticed the uncanny links between her life and the present day. Kyky's fever, his cough, the insect bite, all sounded spookily like Grandad's malaria and infected lungs. Even the normal things that anyone could relate to, like the cold weather and worries about health and friendship, felt oddly apt.

Yet when I finally turned the light out, it wasn't curses I was thinking about: it was adults who pushed you into being someone bigger than you wanted to be. And best friends and brothers, neither of which I had, but which would probably make life a lot better.

*

The next day Tulip wasn't in school again. How she got

away with it, I didn't know. So, at the end of the day, I headed to Highgate to fetch my satchel. From St Kilda's it was a half-hour walk to 24 Makepeace Avenue, which was the address written inside her bag. Desperate as I was to get the jar back, I was also looking forward to seeing Tulip and Oz again.

The road itself was lined with trees so even before I saw Number 24, I knew it was going to be posh. It was halfway along the street. And by crikey, it *was* fancy! I stopped at the gate for a moment just to brush any dirt off my coat. The house was made of brick, with doors arched like a church. Even the windows were beautiful, topped with little panes of blue and red glass.

It was all a bit intimidating, mind you, so I took off my school hat before ringing the bell. Almost immediately, the door flew open and there was Tulip. I was suddenly worried she wouldn't remember who I was.

'Lil!' Tulip cried. 'Thank goodness you tracked us down!'

I was surprised – and delighted – at how pleased she seemed to see me.

'Come in! You're just in time for tea!' Tulip held the door open wide, waving me inside.

I went in on tiptoes, afraid of dirtying the floor, which was blue and white, as beautiful as dinner plates. Everything in the hallway looked expensive: dark, heavy furniture, gold-framed mirrors. There was even a telephone. Helping me out of my coat and dumping it on a chair, Tulip took her own satchel from me.

'I need to talk to you!' she hissed urgently.

I was a bit taken aback. 'Oh! All right.'

'When we have tea, I'll give you a sign.' She sounded excited about it too.

By now I guessed she'd been snooping inside my satchel, and knew about the jar. Instead of feeling miffed, I was rather relieved. Here was a chance to actually talk to someone about it – as long as she could keep a secret.

Tulip took me into a parlour, where Mrs Mendoza was sitting beside the fire, writing. Without her hat, she looked younger – and blonder, her hair fashionably bobbed.

'Mama!' Tulip gushed. 'Lil's come to my rescue by bringing my bag back!'

'Why thank you, Lil. If only we'd had your address, we could've returned yours,' Mrs Mendoza said, smiling.

I was glad she didn't have it, frankly. After seeing where the Mendozas lived, the thought of Tulip coming to our tiny flat made my toes curl with embarrassment.

As Tulip was asked to call Oz down for tea, I was invited to sit on a plush velvet sofa that squeaked when I moved. I couldn't help gazing at all the paintings on the walls – slapdash, scruffy ones that Dad would say a child had done but which were probably very modern.

With a fed-up sigh, Mrs Mendoza closed the notebook she'd been writing in and turned her attention to me. 'Editors are put on this earth to test us, Lil.'

I supposed an editor was someone in charge of writers, and replied: 'My mum works in Woolworths and she says her boss is a cow.'

'Really?' Mrs Mendoza's mouth twitched with a smile. 'Mr Pemberton – my editor – is over here from the States – he works for the *Washington Post*, as do I.'

So she was American? It'd explain her accent. And the way she spoke – freely, as if we were very old pals – put me more at ease.

'What are you writing about?' I asked.

She laughed, though I hadn't meant to be funny. 'The Egyptian dig, of course! Howard Carter inching closer to a big discovery! Is there any other news story worth considering?'

My heart sank: no, there probably wasn't. 'Do you think they'll find the tomb this time?'

'Apparently Mr Carter has narrowed down his search to a particular spot in the valley,' she confided. 'Word has it they're *days* from a discovery!'

I gulped. 'Really?' This wasn't good news at all. If Mr Carter's digging had triggered off the curse like I'd supposed, then I didn't have long to get the jar back to Egypt before Grandad's bad luck – and health – took a further turn for the worse.

Mrs Mendoza was looking equally unhappy.

'Journalists from all over the world are being sent to Egypt to cover the story. I begged my editor to send me – *begged*.' She gritted her teeth. 'But he chose Mr Richards, as usual, and now *he's* had a motorcar accident in Italy.'

'Crumbs!'

'Oh, he's only broken a leg and banged his head.' She batted away my concern. 'The point is Mr Pemberton is now sending another reporter to replace him.'

'Why not you?'

'Reporting on the discovery of a lost pharaoh's tomb?' she scoffed. 'The biggest news story since the end of the war? Why, *that's* a job for a man!'

'What TOSH!' I burst out.

Mrs Mendoza eyed me with what I hoped was respect. 'You took the words out of my mouth.'

Tulip returned then with Oz, who sank into the

chair furthest from any of us. The tea arrived next, plates of hot buttered crumpets, lemon cake, chocolate cake, tiny meringues. I took two of everything, at which Tulip looked shocked, then made flapping gestures as I ate. She was, I soon realised, trying to hurry me up. It was a shame to bolt down such a top tea, but this was obviously *the sign* I'd been told to look out for.

'Let's fetch your satchel, Lil,' Tulip said in a bright voice. 'Oz, you can come too.'

Oz leapt from his chair. I glanced longingly at my crumpets and all the cake I'd not yet tried. But the glare Tulip was giving me made me put my plate aside.

*

We went across the hall to the library. It was amazing that Tulip's house had a room just for books. There were pictures on the walls in here too, though mostly of the same person, a boy with hair that seemed to be constantly falling into his eyes.

'Is that Alex, your brother?' I asked. Even though he was blond and pale-skinned, he looked familiar – a bit like Tulip, I supposed.

She chewed her lip, suddenly serious. 'It is. He went to France in August 1918 and never came home.'

61

I felt awful for mentioning him. 'Gosh … um … I'm sorry.'

''S all right.' Tulip gestured at the silver cups on the shelves, the sort people got at school for sport or writing clever essays. 'Alex was one of those super-brilliant people who won absolutely *everything*, though his luck didn't last forever.'

Oz had started tapping his fingers against his knee in an agitated fashion. Tulip, seeming keen to change the subject, handed me my satchel, which had been hanging from a chair.

'I didn't mean to look inside,' she said, a bit shame-faced. 'I didn't even realise it wasn't mine until last night. But I couldn't sleep with it in my room, not with that jar inside. It really spooked me.'

I was glad I wasn't the only one to have felt this, though being reminded of it made me uneasy too.

'I think it's cursed,' I admitted.

Tulip shuddered. 'Crikey, how gripping!'

'Believe me, it's not,' I said. 'My grandad's poorly in hospital and if he's going to get better, then I've got to return the jar to where it belongs.'

I explained about Grandad and Professor Hanawati being in Egypt together. 'My grandad never wanted to bring the jar back to England, but the professor did, and realised too late that it was cursed.'

'Death shall come on swift wings to anyone who disturbs the grave of a pharaoh,' Tulip said in a dramatic voice.

'Is that a proper saying?' I asked, because I'd not heard it before.

Tulip nodded. 'Someone found it, engraved on a stone, very near to where Mr Carter is digging. Mama told me.'

It sounded unnervingly close to what had happened to the professor and made me shiver.

Oz, meanwhile, was getting impatient.

'Can we *please* talk about the jar?' he begged, shirtsleeves rolled up like he was about to start some sort of task. 'I've inspected it. The stopper is an Anubis head. Its animal form is meant to be that of a jackal, commonly found in the deserts where the dead would've been buried.'

Tulip winked at me. 'I should've warned you, Lil. When my brother gets his teeth into a subject he becomes a walking encyclopaedia.'

'Professor Hanawati reckoned it was a canopic jar,' I said.

'Looks like one,' Oz agreed.

'Aren't those what they put the dead person's lungs and liver and bits and pieces into?' Tulip asked, pulling a face.

'It is,' I said. 'But this jar had a scroll inside, not innards.'

'Can we see?' Tulip peered over my shoulder. 'Open it up, Oz. That jackal-head part looks like it's the lid.'

Just as I'd done, Oz tried to open it. Watching him twist it, then pull it, made me jumpy, though, and in the end I had to take it from him, because I was terrified he'd break it. 'The lid won't budge. I've tried, honest I have.'

'Is the scroll in there still?' Tulip wanted to know.

'Don't think so,' I said. 'Professor Hanawati was translating it when he died.'

'I wonder what it said.' Tulip sighed.

'We should read it,' Oz agreed. 'It might tell us who the jar belonged to.'

I took a deep breath. 'Actually, I have read it – well, the first part of it. He sent the translation to my grandad, with a letter explaining about the curse.'

'And?' Tulip raised an eyebrow. 'Was I right to quote that phrase? Is it from the grave of a pharaoh?'

I looked at Tulip. At Oz. I had to tell them. 'It's about the last days of Tutankhamun – by a girl who actually *knew* him. She calls him Kyky. He was best friends with her brother.'

Tulip blinked. Oz seemed to hold his breath. You

could've heard a spider walk across the room. The amazed look on their faces reminded me – as if I needed it – of the hugeness of what I'd found.

'This is a *really big* discovery, isn't it?' I said, aware of a watery sensation in my stomach.

'You could say that!' Tulip half laughed, half gasped. 'And you've got to send the jar back to Egypt?'

I nodded. 'To a hotel called the Winter Palace where Mr Ibrahim will take care of it.'

'You can't *post* something this valuable to Egypt!' Oz looked horrified. 'You've got to take it to the British Museum!'

'It doesn't belong here,' Tulip tried to explain. 'Professor Hanawati brought it to England by mistake – Lil's just said so.'

'But it should be on display where people can see it,' he persisted.

'In Egypt, maybe, but not here,' I argued. Actually, I didn't think it should be in *any* museum *anywhere* – that was why it was cursed.

'The jar's rightful place is back in Egypt, in Kyky's tomb,' I explained very firmly. 'And that's where it has to go, otherwise my grandad will probably die.'

'I still don't think you should post it,' Oz mumbled.

This was getting frustrating.

'Look, the Winter Palace is a smart hotel in Luxor,' Tulip said. 'But I have to say I've never heard of a Mr Ibrahim.'

I frowned. 'How d'you know all this?'

'It's the hotel where all the reporters covering Mr Carter's story are staying. I've seen the address on telegrams Mama sends.'

'If only your mum was going there now.' I sighed. 'Then we could ask her to take the jar.'

'But Mr Pemberton's sending another reporter,' Oz reminded us.

Tulip had a point about Mr Ibrahim too. We couldn't rely on him to still be working at the Winter Palace. It was over twenty years ago that Grandad was there.

He'd also said that to really understand Egypt, you had to see it for yourself.

'Your mum should go anyway,' I said, thinking out loud. 'Just to prove her editor wrong, and show him how good a writer she is.'

I'd only meant it as a throwaway comment, but Tulip jumped on it straight away. 'Crikey, you're right! If she went she'd insist on taking us with her!'

'What if we faked a telegram from her editor?' I said, warming to the idea. 'What if we made her think he'd changed his mind and sent her instead?'

There'd be train tickets to book, hotels to organise. And we were just a bunch of kids. I didn't know if we could pull it off. Or how quickly.

Tulip narrowed her eyes: it was, I was learning, her 'thinking' look. 'You'd come with us, wouldn't you?'

I almost laughed. '*Me?* I'd love to, but my parents couldn't afford it. I'd have to trust you two.'

'What if someone else were to pay for your ticket?'

Sadly, I shook my head. It wasn't just the money. Apart from a day trip to Southend, I'd never been outside of London. Egypt was the stuff of dreams – the stuff of *Grandad*, who'd always been the adventurous one in our family. My parents weren't like that. They worked hard, kept our rooms tidy, cooked a roast on Sundays if Mum could get a cheap cut of meat. That was their life – it was my life too. And it was far better than some. To wish for anything different felt ungrateful, somehow.

Anyway, Dad would never let me miss weeks of school. And Mum would worry for all of England that I'd catch malaria or some other nasty illness.

No, the closest I'd ever get to going to Egypt was hearing Grandad's stories on a Saturday afternoon over a glass of *chai*.

'I'm sorry,' I said finally. 'It's impossible. I'll have to do what I can here in England.'

After much debate, I was given the job of sending the telegram that would summon Mrs Mendoza to Egypt.

'And I'll pretend to be from the *Washington Post* and book the tickets,' Tulip declared. 'I'll do it over the telephone in my best grown-up voice, then fetch them from the travel agent in person.'

'You can do all *that*?' I was amazed.

'Don't look so worried. Mama often asks me to call them for her if she's rushing off somewhere. It's very easy, I promise you.'

And I bet it was for her. She had a way of just opening her mouth and the right words came out in the proper order. Not to mention the charming, easy smile, so like her mother's, that probably won people over before she'd even spoken. With Tulip on board I began to believe this crazy plan of ours might be possible.

'All right,' I said, with a nervous gulp. 'Let's give it a try.'

7

I'd assumed we'd get cracking on our plan straight away, but in our excitement, we'd forgotten it was the weekend. And that meant fewer trains, closed post offices and our parents at home an annoying amount of the time. We could do very little before Monday, which was hugely frustrating.

'You all right, Lil?' Mum kept asking all Friday night.

'Fine.' But I was pretty useless at keeping secrets, and by Saturday morning, I felt twitchier than ever. I'd also realised the flaw in our plan: Tulip and Oz were returning the jar to a tomb they didn't actually know the whereabouts of.

I was pretty sure by now that it didn't come from Mr Carter's dig. Returning it there to break the curse would be pointless; we'd be taking it from one archaeologist's hands and putting it straight into another's. The evidence pointed to it being somewhere in the Luxor area, but where *exactly*?

What we needed was the rest of Professor Hanawati's translation, which hopefully might tell us where Kyky was buried. I was already keen to read more about Lysandra and Maya, and what happened to poor Kyky in the end: the more I thought about it, the more pressing it became to get hold of the translation. Trouble was, it was very likely to be inside Professor Hanawati's house.

*

'It's not exactly stealing,' Tulip reassured me a few hours later, as we crossed the park in the middle of Russell Square. 'More like collecting what he meant to send to your grandad.'

Directly after breakfast, I'd made excuses about needing a library book, then gone straight to Tulip and Oz's house. Luckily, Tulip had that morning received her pocket money, which covered our bus fares to Russell Square. Professor Hanawati's house was just around the corner.

'But we've still got to get inside the building,' I reminded her.

'Knock on the door,' Oz said, like we'd overlooked something obvious.

'And say what, exactly?' Because I knew I'd go completely tongue-tied.

'I could pretend to be a relative,' Tulip mused. 'Though I'll be surprised if there's anyone at home.'

'In which case, can't I just crawl in through a window?' I said, which felt far more straightforward to me.

'In broad daylight? In central London?' Tulip looked horrified. 'Do you want to go to prison?'

I got the sinking feeling that I'd not thought this through.

At the edge of the park we stopped. It was yet another bitterly cold, grey November day, and it made me wonder vaguely if feast days to the sun actually worked, and whether we should try it some time. We huddled together for warmth – at least, Tulip and I did. Oz stood apart, hands deep in his pockets.

'Which house is his?' Tulip asked, scanning the rows of tall buildings surrounding us on all sides.

'It's down that side street.' I pointed to a turning on the right. The professor's address had been on the letter he'd sent Grandad. 'Number ten.'

It was obvious which house it was – a policeman had been stationed outside. Our chances of getting inside, already slim, now seemed about as likely as a heatwave in December.

It wouldn't have occurred to me in a million years

to approach the policeman, but Tulip was quite composed. 'Let's see what we can find out from him.'

'Are you sure?' I asked warily.

'Lil,' she said. 'Trust me.'

I glanced at Oz, who did a funny half shrug. 'All right.'

We headed down the side street. The policeman, when he saw us coming, rocked back on his heels. Straight away Tulip took charge.

'Can you help us, please? We're supposed to be visiting…' Rummaging in her coat pocket, she pulled out a crumpled bit of paper. I was close enough to see it was a receipt from a bookshop, but bold as brass, she pretended to read out an address. 'My uncle lives there. I'm in the right street, aren't I?'

'He's expecting us, you see,' I chipped in.

'Number ten? Your uncle?' The policeman rubbed his chin.

I worried she'd gone a bit far. But the policeman, taking in Tulip's dark complexion, was clearly of the opinion that if two people had brown skin then they must be related. In short, he believed her.

'This might be a shock to you,' the policeman said. 'But I'm afraid your uncle has passed away.'

'Oh! My goodness!' Tulip wiped her eyes: there

might even have been real tears in them. She'd also, cunningly, kept moving closer to the house's front steps. 'Is my aunt at home? She'd never forgive us if we didn't pay our respects.'

But the policeman was getting suspicious.

'The house is under investigation. You can't go in,' he replied, beckoning us away from the door. 'So I'm afraid you'd best hop it, kiddies.'

*

'He'd never have let you inside,' Oz told Tulip once we were safely out of earshot. 'He probably hasn't even got a key.'

'You still could've backed me up,' she said crossly.

'Thanks for trying, anyway,' I told her.

But we weren't any closer to getting our hands on the translation. I was feeling cold and rather fed up. At this rate, we'd have to wait till after dark to sneak inside the house, and by then our parents would be wondering where we were.

I was mulling all this over when a coal merchant's horse and cart swung out into the street. It'd come from an alleyway alongside the last house in the row. If, as I was thinking, it was a tradesman's entrance, the alley would run along the back of the whole terrace.

It gave me an idea, which I quickly explained to the others.

'You're mad,' Tulip said, though she didn't try and talk me out of it, which I took to be a good sign.

When the policeman was looking the other way, we ducked down the alley. True enough, it ran along the backs of the houses. The plan was for Tulip and Oz to stay near the entrance and keep watch.

'Don't be long!' Tulip whispered.

I'd once heard it said that thieves would spend hours watching a house they planned to rob, but we didn't have that luxury.

'I'll time you,' Oz said, looking at his watch. 'Ten minutes. Go!'

I set off, aiming for the third house in the row. What I hoped to find was a little larder window left open or a cellar door unlocked. I was nervous, and was sure it looked obvious to everyone that I was up to no good.

Almost immediately a servant girl came out of the first house to throw potato peelings in a bin. She glared at me, hands on hips. 'You better not be one of them newspaper reporters, sniffing around here again.'

She must've had terrible eyesight to mistake me for a grown-up.

'I've lost my dog.' It was the first thing I could think of.

'Aye, that's what they all say,' she sneered, but thankfully went back inside.

By the time I got to the right house, I was sweating. I'd visions of the Hanawatis' maid chasing after me with a broom, or their cook threatening me with a rolling pin. But the back of the place was completely shut up and silent. There were no lights on inside, no smoke coming from the chimneys. Steps led to a basement, so with a quick glance over my shoulder, I went down them, and found the door at the bottom locked.

Somewhere out in the lane, I heard another door slam, and voices – a girl's and a man's – coming from the opposite end to where Tulip and Oz were keeping watch.

'She's down here somewhere, poking about,' the girl said. I recognised her voice and groaned: it was the short-sighted servant again.

'You did the right thing, coming to find me. Now leave this in the hands of the law,' the man reassured her.

I gulped: the *law*? Drat and blast it! The stupid girl had only gone and fetched the policeman from round the front.

Flustered, I tried the basement door again. It was still locked. No amount of rattling and pushing would change it. Nor was there time to run. Already I could see the top of the policeman's helmet as he approached the house next door. Desperately, I tried to think up an excuse for being here – the dog one obviously hadn't worked.

When I saw the coal-chute door, all thinking stopped. It was at head height next to the basement entrance, and metal. And more importantly, when I lifted the hatch, it was just about big enough. This was my way in.

With a great heave and a kick, I scrambled through the opening. The hatch swung shut behind me. The policeman must've thought I'd vanished into thin air.

The chute part was short. I slid down it chin first and hit the ground with a whump. It was pretty dark down here, and stank of damp and coal, though thankfully the floor was a soil one and soft, so I wasn't hurt. I scrambled to my feet.

The door from the coal store led out on to a brick passage. Down one end was the kitchen: the only sound coming from it was that of a dripping tap. At the other end was a staircase that I guessed led to the ground floor. I sprang up the stairs. Though I could feel my heart beating strongly, I wasn't scared any more. I'd done the hard bit. I'd got inside. All I had to do now was find the translation and crawl back up the coal chute.

In the hallway, I hesitated: where to look first?

In his letter to Grandad, the professor had mentioned a study and working at a desk.

The study was the first room I came to, though finding it wasn't down to luck. What got my attention was a terrible smell. On opening the door, the smell got ten times worse, so bad in fact that I had to cover my mouth with my hand. It was worse than a meat locker in summer. Worse than our outside lav when the drains blocked up. It was so bad, I couldn't put a name to it.

The room itself felt strange too, the air prickly, as if someone had been in here only seconds ago. For the first time since coming into the house, I began to feel ill at ease. Though the shutters were closed at the windows there was enough light to see by: everything looked black and grey. At the centre of the room was a desk – smaller than Grandad's and definitely tidier. A blotter, a stack of notebooks and a letter rack were all lined up neatly down one side. A jacket had been slung across the chair, like someone had just taken it off. It made me suddenly sad, that jacket: I tried very hard not to look at it, instead keeping my eyes peeled for any sign of Professor Hanawati's distinctive royal-blue writing paper.

A couple of steps to the left and I realised I'd trodden in something horrid. In the gloom I couldn't see what, but the soles of my shoes were sticking to it. Lifting my feet made a slurpy, wet sound, and the smell, if it was possible, got worse. I couldn't tell where it was coming from, only that it filled the whole room and made my stomach heave.

Quickly now, I searched the professor's desk. There were no letters. The notebooks were mostly empty. The translation wasn't here, either. I just hoped he hadn't hidden it somewhere unlikely. I didn't think my guts could stand this smell much longer.

Next, I searched the bookshelves. Shook out books. Felt between them. Nothing. Then, on a side table, I noticed a photograph in a silver frame.

In the picture were two men – one I didn't recognise, with a dark, proud face, and the other I did: it was Grandad. The photograph was taken in the desert – Egypt, I guessed – and though the jar wasn't in the shot, like an invisible force, you could sense the damage was already at work. Professor Hanawati – for that was who the other man was, I was certain – looked angrily at the camera. Grandad stared at the ground.

It was a shock to see them both as young, unhappy men. But it was nothing compared to what I saw next. When I'd first come into the room, the desk had blocked it out. Now the hearth rug lay before me in all its gruesome glory.

There was something on it. Something dark and grey that looked like cinders from the fire. The once pretty carpet was now completely blackened, yet the armchair right next to it hadn't even been scorched.

Come to think of it, the ashes weren't like ones from a fire. They were darker, heavier, with a smell like bad meat. I felt clammy and sicker than ever, because I'd read the newspaper report, so I knew exactly what I was looking at. The article had described the hearth rug in horrid detail. This was the very room, the very spot where Professor Hanawati had burned to death.

Someone had tried to clear away the mess: the one small mercy was the feet had gone. But my brain still couldn't cope with what I was seeing.

I didn't know if I was going to be sick or faint. I couldn't stay in this room any longer. As I turned to go, at the very last moment, I spotted the corner of a piece of bright blue paper sticking out from under the armchair. I hesitated: it was right next to the ashes.

Holding my breath, I ducked down. Grabbed it quick. And it was paper – more than one piece – with the title 'Lysandra', and completely untouched by the fire. I'd never been so glad to see anything in my life.

Stuffing it down my coat, and before I breathed another breath, I ran for the door.

LYSANDRA

The feast day dawns with a clear blue sky. Kyky has chosen his favourite horses for the chariot race: Lion, a young chestnut, and Myrrh whose black coat ripples like water. Sensing excitement in the air, they refuse to keep still as I try to plait their tails.

Roti the stable boy admires my handiwork. 'I'd bet my finest blanket on those horses winning!'

Most of the wagers are on the king himself, Roti tells me. In the palace courtyard, under the fig trees, crowds are gathering to place their bets. A medicine woman is offering to pull out bad teeth for free. There are bottles of sandalwood, heeled shoes, puppies, a song to charm snakes. The queen has bet her finest earrings, so loaded with rubies they make the wearer's earlobes stretch.

The sun is shining, the air is warm. Amun is smiling down on us again. It is a day for being happy, I tell myself, yet it does little to calm my nerves.

The race is scheduled for mid-afternoon. A crowd lines the route which runs from the palace, through the marketplace down to the river, before looping back past the temple with its newly built ram-headed sphinxes. It's turned into a hot day. Mother and I are wearing white tunics, and kohl under our eyes to beat the glare. We take our spot outside the palace gates where the race will start and end.

'Maya could win,' Mother says proudly, but under her breath.

'The king always wins,' I remind her.

When the two chariots appear it's not hard to see why. Maya looks almost too big for his vehicle. All arms and legs, he's struggling to keep his balance. His horses, Bes and Beetle, have grazed too much winter grass on the riverbanks, and are plump next to Kyky's pair.

Kyky, in contrast, is regal. He too has kohl painted thickly on his eyelids. He's wearing a gold headdress, and a breastplate bright with jewels. His horses, I think smugly, are exquisite. They're snorting and shaking their manes, pawing the dust. In this rare moment when he truly looks like a pharaoh Kyky's the obvious winner.

On the palace steps, Horemheb the army general starts the race. Behind him, seated, is Ay. Kyky glances at his godfather, raises his hand – wish me luck, that little wave says. Ay nods, then looks away. It makes me sad for Kyky, whose devotion to his godfather is never quite returned.

All eyes are on Horemheb now as he holds aloft a bronze gong. Excitement shimmers through the crowd. As he thumps the instrument, it booms. There's a fraction of a moment when neither Kyky nor Maya moves. Then the creak of wood, reins snapping against horses' necks and dust everywhere as the chariots surge forwards. A terrific roar goes up from the crowd.

Mother grips my arm: I grip hers. We stand locked together.

As the dust clears we see the back of Kyky's chariot speeding down the street. Despite the bumps and holes, he's going steadily. Maya is some way behind. He's shouting at his horses, at Kyky to slow down. The crowd laughs; they're loving it.

When the chariots are out of sight, the crowd goes

after them. A great wave of people jostling, necks craning, blood buzzing.

'Keep up, Mother!' I hold out my hand to her. She laughs as she stumbles, then catches hold of me again.

In the marketplace the stalls have been pushed aside. The road is wide, dipping gently down to the river. Up ahead, blocking the route, is a heap of rubble. Not so long ago it was a statue to the old god Aten. Now it's a hazard. Kyky throws all his weight to one side. The chariot swerves just in time to avoid it.

Maya, lumbering behind, does the same move. His weight is greater. I cry out as his chariot tips. One wheel leaves the ground, then, magically, it is righted again. I think I've squeezed all the blood from Mother's hand.

By the time the chariots reach the river, we've lost sight of them. Mother and I, and most of the crowd, walk back to the palace where the race will finish. Every now and then, we hear a distant cheer, a groan.

It's frustrating not to see what's happening. At first people are impatient, standing on tiptoe. But as time passes, the crowd settles again. In the middle of the street, doves peck the dirt. A hungry dog, who's been

83

watching them, lies down and goes to sleep.

I start to worry. It can't take this long to gallop around our town. Something must have gone wrong. I go over Kyky's dream again, the darkness, the wild animals, and feel that same coldness in my veins.

Mother nudges me: 'Look.'

On the palace steps, Horemheb is pointing in the direction of the temple.

'They return!' he bellows. 'Everyone stand back!'

Eager to catch first sight of them, we press to the sides of the road. I can hear hoofbeats now. I'm excited again. On tiptoe, straining to see.

In the distance I hear rumbling chariot wheels. There's dust in the air, coming towards us like a sandstorm. Shouts. The smell of sweating horses. The doves fly up in panic. The dog awakes and skulks off into the crowd.

The road is empty. Then it isn't.

It's Maya I see first. He's crouched forwards, almost touching Bes and Beetle's rumps. Kyky isn't far behind. Soon he's level with Maya again. By the time they reach us, they're at full gallop. All I see is a blur of speed: brown horses, brown chariots, brown dust. The finish line is just ahead. Up on the palace steps, Horemheb gets ready to bang his gong.

The dust clears enough to see Kyky edge ahead. Maya's horses are tiring. He makes a show of urging them on, but the race is over. The king's going to win. We all laugh with delight. There's cheering and clapping.

Then comes an almighty crash. The sound of splintering wood. A stunned silence because we all know this isn't meant to happen. People start screaming. The whole crowd pushes and heaves in different directions.

'Is someone hurt?' Mother cries.

I'm almost too terrified to look.

There's a chariot on its side in the road. Two horses are struggling to get up. When I realise they're not Bes and Beetle, I sob with relief. But if it's not Maya, then it must be Kyky.

'No, Lysandra, stay back,' Mother pleads.

I squirm free of her grasp, reaching the broken chariot just as Maya does. Kyky has been thrown from the vehicle. He lies some distance away, face down in the dust. People are crowding around him now, unsure what to do or whether to move him.

No order comes from the palace steps. Ay hasn't got up from his seat. Horemheb is at his shoulder, talking angrily to him.

85

It's Maya who gives the orders.

'Take him inside,' he says to the strongest-looking people in the crowd. 'Be careful of his head and leg.'

As Kyky is lifted up, the injuries are clear. His leg is at an odd angle. There's a gash on his head. But his eyes are opening: he's alive!

Sinking to my knees to thank the gods, I see the chariot wheel, lying in the dirt. I wonder why no one else has noticed it. Two spokes are broken. The whole thing is buckled beyond repair.

I was there this morning when Roti checked everything, then checked it all again. He wouldn't have missed damage like this. He wouldn't put the king's life at risk.

No, he wouldn't, I think, my gaze resting on the palace steps, but there are those who would. If the pharaoh dies, Ay is the next living male heir. This, I think bitterly, means Kyky is worth more to his ambitious godfather dead than alive.

The healing ladies spend the next day tending to Kyky. From our house we see pots and baskets carried in – fresh incense, linens, herbs and potions. The more I think about how the right wheel sheared off, the more certain I am it was deliberate. Ay, keen to place *blame, has already found his target. Poor Roti was dragged from the stables last night and beaten with his own horsewhip.*

Maya brings us news as we're closing the shutters against the midday sun. He confirms my thoughts. 'Kyky's head wound is deep – to the bone. They've bound up his leg in case it's fractured. He's very lucky – he could've been killed.'

Maya's one of the few allowed at Kyky's bedside. It's not nearly as much fun as hurling pomegranates or hunting ostrich, but he shows equal devotion to it.

'He's blessed to have such a friend,' I say.

'He's asking for you, Lysandra.'

Mama stares. I'm suddenly chilled. I'm certain he wants to talk more about his dream.

Kyky's bedchamber is in the coolest part of the palace. It catches the breeze from the river, and facing north-east it gets only the earliest rays of sun.

Kyky is awake. His eyes are night-dark from the medicine he's taken, though I'm not sure if it's helping much. He's fidgety and irritable.

'Leave us!' he tells the healing ladies who crouch at the edges of the room.

Kyky doesn't speak again until he's very sure we're alone, and even then he lowers his voice. I wonder who he thinks might be out there, eavesdropping. It's not hard to guess.

'Lysandra, the conversation we had – about my dream,' Kyky says. 'You haven't told anyone, have you?'

'Just Maya,' I reply, who probably knew about it before I did.

'Good. I don't want people to think me weak.'

'Weak?' I'm startled. So is Maya when I catch his eye. 'There's no taint in dream reading. It's a tradition as old as the hills—'

Kyky interrupts: 'A window into the afterlife, yes, I know what it means, but everyone assumes I'm dying.'

'You told me the door in your dream was closed,' I remind him. 'You're not ready for that journey yet.'

'Ah! But I came close to it yesterday, didn't I?'

There are parts of his dream that concern me, yes. He is in danger from something. Or someone.

'Perhaps yesterday wasn't an accident, after all,' I confess.

Kyky frowns. 'The stable boy was slack in his work, so I heard.'

'It wasn't his fault,' I argue. 'He checked your chariot before the race and there was nothing wrong. Someone else must've tampered with it.'

I glance at Maya, hoping he'll agree. But he's pacing the room, as alert as a snake. He stops in front of one of the windows, gestures for us to be quiet. I hold my breath as he listens at the shutters, then flings them open in one swift movement. We all hear the patter of feet as whoever was out there listening runs away.

'Kyky's right,' Maya says. 'No more talk of dreams.'

We don't talk of the accident again, either. By the time the moon's waned, Kyky's hobbling around the palace as if nothing happened. He's cut himself a new walking stick to mark the occasion. Word is he's also trying to show more interest in the running of the kingdom. I wonder what Ay and Horemheb make of this change.

One night in the orange glow of Mama's cooking fire, Maya takes me aside to tell me the new arrangement isn't going well.

'They don't listen to him,' he confesses. 'All the decisions still come from Ay or Horemheb. When they can't agree, they bribe Kyky for his support.'

'But you're there at these meetings. Can't you speak up for him?' I ask.

'I won't be there any more. From tomorrow, I've been ordered out into the desert to find a site for Kyky's tomb.'

This worries me. 'Is he sick again?'

Maya shakes his head. 'He's healing well. But Ay says we should've started work on it years ago. It takes time and sweat to build a tomb fit for a pharaoh.'

This is true: Kyky's mother, father and beloved grandmother all have lavish golden chambers hewn from the desert floor. Their journeys onward to the next life will have been comfortable. Easy. Maya's right to want the same luxuries for Kyky.

Yet I can't shake off the fact that Ay is behind this. The wayward chariot wheel, ears pressed to window shutters, the building of a grave. Nothing is what it seems.

After a few days of searching, Maya finds the perfect site for the tomb. He comes home at sundown, exhausted but thrilled.

'What's it like, the spot you've picked?' I ask.

'I'll take you,' he says to my surprise.

Mother insists I wear sandals because of scorpions

or snakes. I don't like anything on my feet, but for this it's a small price to pay. Since Kyky's dream I've been wary of anything with a poisonous bite.

Beyond the city wall the desert stretches in all directions. We go west, heading towards a place where river waters used to run. Nowadays, it's a dry valley, the sides of which are almost sheer rock. I know the spot well – it's only a short walk from Thebes. It is where people of power and prestige are taken after death to begin their journey to the world beyond.

Maya walks with huge, raking strides. I keep asking him to slow down. We slither down a path, already worn into the hillside by the men working with Maya.

'Which way?' I ask, when we reach the point where the valley divides.

'East,' Maya replies.

I'm surprised: west-facing graves are more favoured because they catch the setting sun.

After a steep climb, the tomb site comes into view. It's a few hundred feet up the cliff face, set back from the edge. Ropes and baskets and other signs of work litter the ground below. Already they've made good progress – I can see steps cut from the rock. The view out over the valley is magnificent. I'm proud of my *thoughtful brother. This is a beautiful place to be at rest. My brother is smiling, though, shaking his head as though I've not quite understood.*

'It's only the beginning,' he says. 'If my measurements are correct then the real beauty will come from the sun.'

PART THREE

The shadows move but the dark is never completely dispersed.

HOWARD CARTER, ARCHAEOLOGIST

8

That night in bed my brain kept whizzing. You did it, Lil, I told myself. You found the translation. But it wasn't the end of the story, was it? There was no mention of how Kyky died, or his funeral or the burial, which made me think there was still more to this account, even now.

Then there was the curse. Kyky's injuries from the chariot accident were too similar to those of the *Washington Post*'s reporter who'd crashed his car. Head injuries, fractured legs – it was no coincidence. Anyone with a special interest in the Tutankhamun story seemed to be at risk from the curse. And that included us.

I lay there, my heart booming, thinking this over. At least the translation *did* give us a better idea of where Kyky's tomb might be. The accounts of Mr Carter's dig said his search was on the valley floor, yet Maya's chosen place was high up in the rock face. It suggested two tombs, then, not one.

It was bizarre to think Mr Carter himself didn't know this. But then, didn't the professor say that Mr Carter had dismissed the jar as 'insignificant' all those years ago?

He'd be kicking himself now.

Yet as far as the newspapers were concerned, he was already a national hero. Which made me remember something Grandad said:

'They called King Louis XIV of France the Sun King because of how important he thought he was. His mission in life? To dazzle everyone. Yet don't forget, Lily, underneath those wigs and gold brocade, he was just a man with flat feet and bad breath. That Howard Carter, he's like a sun king. Everyone thinks he's a go-getting explorer, but he's a sly one, mark my words. He's got secrets by the bagful.'

*

I wondered how Mr Carter managed to keep his secrets to himself. All weekend I tried my very best to keep our plans secret. But by Sunday it was getting exhausting.

'What's wrong with that last spud, Lil?' Dad asked as we ate our roast lunch.

'Nothing.' I shoved it in my mouth quick before he could pinch it. I mean, it was a very decent lunch. We had lamb, potatoes done in lard, carrots, tinned peas and gravy thick as treacle. Mum was good at roasts, but this one was especially nice, almost as if we were celebrating something. Even I, with my head full of Egypt, couldn't fail to notice.

When lunch was finished, I went down to swill our dishes under the tap in the back yard, and when I came upstairs again, Mum and Dad were discussing me. Since the kitchen door was ajar, I hovered there to listen.

'She could come with us, Reg,' Mum was saying. 'It might be nice to do it as a family this year.'

'What about her schoolwork?' Dad replied. 'St Kilda's won't tolerate her falling behind. I wonder sometimes if she realises just how lucky she is?'

I groaned. St Kilda's *again*. The work I had to do, the gratitude I was expected to show. Dad never seemed to talk about anything else.

Except then he said, 'We agreed never to tell her, remember?'

'She's older now,' Mum pointed out.

I was all ears: what *were* they on about? It didn't sound like St Kilda's any more.

The kitchen door opened fully. Dad came out, saw me and for a second looked almost lost.

'There you are!' he said, forcing a smile. His hands were shaking badly. Seeing I'd noticed he quickly stuffed them in his pockets.

'Dishes are done,' I muttered.

'Good girl. Your mother and I are popping out for a stroll, all right? It's best that you stay here and get your prep done.'

*

The second my parents left, I slumped face down amongst my schoolbooks. I couldn't concentrate. I was now anxious about where they'd gone. They never went out together. Dad went to the pub on a Friday evening and once a month Mum played cribbage with her work pals from Woolworths: that was it.

The only thing I could think was that they'd gone to visit Grandad, though it seemed unlikely. Grandad and Dad couldn't bear to be in the same room as each other. That made me worry even more. If they *had* gone to the hospital, then it must be for the very worst reason, that Grandad was dying and Dad had gone to settle their differences.

On the brink of tears, I got up and put on my coat. If Grandad was that ill then I had to see him too. He must know I was trying my very hardest to get the jar back to Egypt, with my friends' help. If he could just hang on for a few more days, he'd see – though how I'd say all this with Mum and Dad at the bedside I'd no idea.

*

In the street, I soon spotted my parents. I was about to run to catch them up when I realised they'd passed the bus stop. They weren't going to the hospital, after all. What relief I felt quickly turned to confusion, because they were certainly going *somewhere*.

Swithin's Street itself was busy with kids out on their bikes or playing hopscotch on the pavement. After weeks of cold weather, it was a bright, warm day. There were people chatting on doorsteps, a couple of cats stretched out on a wall in the sunshine. It was, all told, a nice afternoon for a stroll.

Yet my parents weren't strolling. Dad was going so fast Mum kept having to break into a run to stay with him. And so did I, as I followed on behind. Just when I could feel a stitch coming on, Dad turned down St Mary's Lane, a little road that ran behind the cutlery factory, before it stopped in a dead end at the churchyard and convent.

We never went to church as a family. Once, when I'd asked why not, Dad replied: 'Passchendaele. No god would've let that happen.'

Today, though, my parents were heading for St Mary's. They had to be. There was nothing else down there. It was a funny little place. Jammed in by the factory wall on one side and the convent on the other, it had the greenest, most overgrown graveyard you ever saw. Long ago, during the Black Death, it'd been a plague pit. Nowadays, it was where you'd see couples on their break from the factory having a quick smoke or a kiss. As far as I knew, neither of these was a reason for my parents to go there. Nor was the obvious one: all the dead people in our family were buried at the big cemetery near the Heath.

By the time I reached St Mary's, they were already in the churchyard. Dad had slowed down and was reaching out to take Mum's hand, making me realise they wanted to be alone. So I hid behind the gatepost.

On either side of the path were ancient gravestones that had fallen over in the long grass or sunk into the soil. I was dying to see which one Mum and Dad would stop in front of. Perhaps an army chum of Dad's was buried here. You often heard about men who'd returned from the war, who despite being back home with their families never recovered from their injuries.

Not too far along the path, they did stop. Mum said something to Dad, who took off his hat and held it to his chest. Then he spoke to her – I couldn't hear what he said, above the blackbirds and trams going by on the main road and someone in a nearby garden calling to their cat.

The strange thing was, neither of them seemed to be looking down at a grave. They were gazing straight ahead at the long whitewashed wall, behind which was the convent. Standing there, they looked different: not their usual weary selves, but so full of emotion they were shaking with it. And it frightened me, rather. I'd never seen them react like this to anything, or anyone, before.

They didn't stay long. On the way out, when they passed my hiding spot, I froze in case they saw me. But they were so lost to their thoughts that neither of them even looked up from the path. All the way back down Swithin's Street, they walked in silence. I followed at a safe distance.

Then, at the bottom of our street, they stopped outside the pub.

'A sweet sherry before closing time?' I heard Dad ask.

It was pretty brazen of him, to be honest. Women round our way didn't go to the pub. It was where men went to escape their wives, and where wives were glad to send them, Mum always said. But that sweet sherry was a godsend, because it gave me a chance to get home before they did.

*

They didn't come back for ages, long enough for my mind to drift to tomorrow, and the telegram I'd be sending. The post office wouldn't open till nine, so I'd have to miss the first lesson, and my St Kilda's uniform, I knew all too well, stuck out like a pimple. This time I decided not to take any chances. Mum, I knew, had a plain black skirt which I could wear then, afterwards, change back into my uniform.

It wasn't that my parents' room was out of bounds – more that it was theirs, not mine. It smelled of Mum, and Dad's hair oil, and sometimes, if the window hadn't been opened in a while, of last night's cooking. It was the only other proper-sized room in our flat. As

I tiptoed through the door, I felt instantly guilty. Mum would've lent me her skirt if I asked. But I couldn't without her wanting to know why.

In the corner of the room was a curtain: behind it, on pegs, hung my parents' few clothes. There was the black skirt, shiny with wear, but what caught my eye was Mum's little cardboard suitcase on the floor beneath. It was covered in dust because no one ever used it. Seeing it there, I thought of Tulip and Oz, who were probably packing for tomorrow's trip right at this moment. I felt envious. Worried. Glad of our crazy plan. As I unhooked the skirt, I let myself dream, just for a second, that I was going with them, and I'd come in here to borrow Mum's suitcase.

I picked it up. Just to try it. Though the handle creaked dryly, it was thrilling to hold. I imagined loading it on to a train or a ferry, and covering it with stickers to show all the countries we'd passed through. I didn't realise the latches on the case weren't clicked shut until the lid swung open, hitting me in the shin.

'Ouch!' I hissed, rubbing my leg.

A piece of paper fell out, fluttering to the floor. It looked like a receipt or a ticket until I picked it up. On it was written:

```
BOY 8 LBS 6 OZ
Born 19th November 1899
St Mary's Convent,
Islington, London
```

An odd feeling crept through me. Somehow, I didn't think I was meant to see this bit of paper. If the dust was anything to go by, it'd been inside the suitcase for years. Nor did it seem a coincidence that 19 November was today's date: the baby's birthday.

Was this why Mum and Dad had gone to St Mary's Convent, or at least stood outside, looking so upset? And was it the reason for our super-special Sunday lunch?

I'd no idea, but my head started reeling. Something was going on here, something shadowy and private. And in my own family too!

Footsteps were coming up the stairs.

Panicking, I pushed the suitcase back in place, grabbed the black skirt and ran. I made it to my bedroom just as the front door opened. Mum and Dad took their coats and hats off, went wearily to the kitchen. The smell of sherry and tobacco trailed behind them, as did I, once I'd hidden the black skirt under my bed.

'Hullo, love,' Mum said, seeing me in the doorway. 'I'll make us all a nice cuppa, shall I?'

'Been working hard, she has, look,' Dad said proudly, pointing at my books on the kitchen table.

'I have,' I agreed.

It was only a half lie. But it came out easily, especially now I wasn't the only one with secrets.

9

The next morning, bright and early, I went to the post office. Deliberately, I chose one nearer to Tulip's house than ours. I didn't want to run into anyone I knew, not when I was in Mum's black skirt and sweating rather badly.

'First nine words are tuppence,' the lady behind the counter said, looking down her nose at me. 'After that it's a penny a word.'

I prayed it wasn't obvious I'd never sent a telegram before. Without my school hat, I might pass as an office junior on an errand, albeit a very young one with clammy hands. I thought how Tulip would be confident, smiling, looking everyone in the eye, and tried my best to do the same.

'Here.' I slid across the money, all in halfpennies.

She counted it, then passed me the form to fill in. Nine words wasn't much. I settled on: 'CHANGE OF PLAN – *STOP* – GO TO LUXOR – *STOP* – TICKETS ON WAY – *STOP* –'

I signed it 'MR PEMBERTON'.

When I'd finished, the post office lady checked it, then sent it off. I tapped my foot nervously in time with the telegram machine.

'When will it be delivered, please?' I asked.

She glanced at her watch. 'I'd give it thirty minutes.'

I couldn't believe it'd been that easy – and that fast.

*

My optimism didn't last, mind you. Halfway down the street, I heard the first of the day's newsboys. It wouldn't have been such a shock had I seen the headline over breakfast, but I'd ducked out this morning, too keyed up to eat.

'Carter discovers tomb steps as hunt for King Tut closes in!'

Panic washed over me. So, he'd found the official tomb – or at least the way in. This was just the sort of development we didn't need. How much longer would it be before Mr Carter dug his way right inside? How – or who – would the curse strike then?

I couldn't shake off the feeling of danger hanging over us. If there was a downside to reading Lysandra's account, this was it: I worried now that almost everything was a sign. I just prayed Tulip's part of our plan had gone as smoothly as mine.

By the time I reached Makepeace Avenue, it was nearly ten o'clock. I'd come to give Tulip the jar and the professor's translations. Thankfully, she answered the front door, grabbing my sleeve and practically dragging me inside.

'Have you seen the news this morning about the tomb steps?' I asked.

She nodded, a finger on her lips, and hurried me to the library. There, she shut the door behind us and leaned against it. She looked rather grim. I perched on the sofa next to Oz, who was biting the skin around his fingernails.

'What's wrong? Has the telegram arrived?' I asked.

'Yes,' Tulip confirmed. 'Though I'm afraid Mama got rather upset.'

My stomach dropped. 'Doesn't she want to go to Luxor?'

'Yes, yes, of course she does,' Tulip quickly reassured me. 'It was just a bit of a shock, seeing the telegram boy's uniform and his red bike, and all that. It reminded her – and us – of the day we got the news that Alex was missing.'

I felt dreadful for not thinking of this; clearly Tulip did too.

She hurried on. 'Anyway, I've picked up the tickets. I'll tell Mama the *Washington Post* sent them.' Fetching an envelope from the table, she waved it triumphantly in the air: 'Train to Athens, boat across to Cairo, another train down to Luxor! I've even booked us in at the Winter Palace Hotel. And return tickets for three weeks' time.'

I whistled. It was incredible what confidence, the right-sounding voice and a telephone could achieve. Tulip was amazing. I was completely in awe, and so very grateful, I felt suddenly choked up.

'It's ... what I mean is ... thank you for what you've done,' I stuttered.

'Don't simper, Lil,' she said, playfully. 'It's not your style.'

But I couldn't have done any of this on my own.

'What if your mum finds out she's paid for everything, though?' I asked, because I still couldn't believe it had all gone so smoothly. 'Won't she go bonkers?'

Tulip rolled her eyes. 'I told you before: everything's on the *Washington Post*'s account, just as usually happens if I'm sorting out a train for Mama.'

I wasn't sure if it was genius or madness, but our crazy little plan was working. 'You're leaving tonight, aren't you?'

'Yes, from St Pancras,' Tulip said. 'The seven o'clock Continental Express to Athens.'

Everything was in place. Tulip, Oz and their mum were travelling on a train, on a boat, all the way across Europe and the Mediterranean to Egypt. How I wished, with every ounce of me, that I was going with them. I couldn't bear to even imagine what that would be like any more.

I took a long slow breath. All that was left to do now was hand over the jar. Opening my satchel, I passed the box to Tulip.

'I've tucked the translations inside,' I told her and Oz.

As she went to take it from me, I felt a sudden twist of fear. What if this wasn't the right thing to do? What if something happened to the jar, or worse, to Oz and Tulip? By asking them to do this for me and for Grandad, had I just passed on the curse to my friends?

'Lil,' Tulip said gently. 'You can let go of the box.'

'Sorry. Here, take it.' It was too late by now to do anything else.

*

By the time I'd changed into my St Kilda's uniform and left Tulip's, it was still only ten thirty. The plan was to slip into class between lessons, unnoticed. I'd hoped Tulip might come with me, but she refused, and quite firmly too.

'Not a chance! I've got clothes to pack!' she said.

Funny how on the subject of school she wasn't her normal confident self. I'd even go so far as to say she was blustering. The packing seemed like an excuse; I suspected there was more to her missing school than she was telling me.

At St Kilda's, I made it all the way through the quad and along the corridor to English before anyone so much as looked at me. Too bad the person who did was Millicent Thorpe, the girl who noticed everything.

'Look what the cat's dragged in,' she said to one of her many shadows – I didn't know her friends' names, just that wherever Millicent went they'd trail behind.

I did my best not to react. And for a while, I managed it. The lesson started with Miss Parker announcing another spelling test – not my favourite pastime by anyone's standards, but for once I had a go at all twenty words, and even did a few doodles in the margin for good measure. I was determined not to be glum.

A girl called Geraldine who sat on the front row was then told to collect our answers. Everyone else was allowed a brief moment to chat.

'How's your new friend, Lilian?' Millicent called out in her snidey, wheedling way.

I ignored her.

'Is she pally with that dark-skinned girl?' someone else asked. 'The one who never comes to school? I swear I saw them together on the bus on Saturday.'

I felt an angry blush creeping up my neck.

'Tulip Mendoza?' This was Millicent. 'Stupid name if you ask me. And have you seen her curly *hair*?'

I spun round in my seat. The whispering stopped. Millicent sat back, arms folded as if to say, *'What're you staring at?'*

I turned to face the front again. They could talk about me all they liked, but now they'd mentioned Tulip I started to get annoyed. I didn't notice Geraldine hovering near my desk to collect my test until she said to the teacher, 'What about Lilian Kaye's paper, miss? She's drawn all over it.'

Before I could stop her, she'd snatched my test and was holding it up for Miss Parker to see. It was only a scribble or two – of Nefertiti mostly – but the whole class went silent. Twenty pairs of eyes stared at me like I'd committed murder.

'If you've defaced your test, Lilian,' Miss Parker said, unimpressed, 'then you'll stay behind after school and redo it.'

I'd not meant to groan out loud. Everyone gasped. I knew then I'd gone too far: St Kilda's students *never* answered back.

Behind me one of Millicent's friends was whispering again: 'Going to call on *Tulip* tonight, are you?'

'Can't think what she'd see in you,' Millicent added. 'She's stinking rich. Mind you, you know what they say about foreigners, and Mendoza isn't an English—'

Something in me snapped. I got up from my seat, flinging my chair back so hard it screeched across the floor. When I stopped in front of Millicent's desk, she still had that stupid mocking look on her face. In a flash, I had hold of her hair. She screamed. Kicking. Yelling at me to let go.

'You say one more thing about Tulip,' I hissed right in her face, 'and I'll tear your stupid plaits off your head.'

'You're insane! You should be locked up!' she cried.

'And you're a nasty bully,' I spat back. 'But you don't scare me. Or Tulip. She's got more courage in her little finger than you and your drippy friends put together.'

I'd have said more too, but Miss Parker was booming my name at the top of her voice.

*

That's how I came to be in the headmistress's office. Though I felt wretched, my only real regret was that I'd not stood up to Millicent Thorpe earlier. Bullies like her were probably the reason why Tulip hated coming to school.

'Who sent you?' Mrs Emerson-Jones, the headmistress, drawled from behind her great sarcophagus of a desk.

'Miss Parker,' I said.

'And your name?'

'Lilian Kaye, miss.'

'What's your misdemeanour, Lilian?' She sounded almost bored.

'Fighting, miss.'

'Fighting, eh?' She looked at me with new interest. 'You're one of our scholarship students, are you not?'

I knew what she was getting at, that my being from a poor family explained why I'd grabbed Millicent Thorpe's hair, because a proper young lady would never do such a thing.

'I didn't start it,' I said. 'They were bad-mouthing Tulip Mendoza—'

Mrs Emerson-Jones interrupted: 'Tulip? The girl who refuses to attend school?'

'Yes, miss. And I reckon I can see why. She's being bullied by that Millicent Thorpe and her pals.'

Mrs Emerson-Jones looked at me like I'd just said the sky was green. 'Bullying? Here, at St Kilda's? I hardly think so!'

'Oh it's true, miss,' I persisted. 'And Tulip's my friend, see, so I'm not going to sit back and ignore it, am I?'

'In my school that's *exactly* what I'd expect you to do,' she huffed. 'You should turn the other cheek.'

But I'd always been told – by Grandad and my parents – that you didn't think less of a person just because they weren't like you. It came from Grandad's travels to other countries, I supposed, and Dad being overseas in the war.

You certainly didn't make fun of someone because of their hair or their skin, or because they wore glasses or lived in the wrong sort of street. That was plain wrong.

'Millicent was saying nasty things about Tulip having dark skin, and it's not right, not from anyone,' I told her.

'Was there not a teacher in the room?' she snapped. 'Could you not have told her?'

I shrugged miserably. 'Maybe, and then I'd have been called a telltale.'

'Instead, you chose to behave like a thug!' Mrs Emerson-Jones exclaimed. 'It won't be tolerated in this school, do you hear?'

My heart sank to the floor. We all knew what the punishment was for fighting, and as Mrs Emerson-Jones opened her desk drawer, I squeezed my eyes shut. I didn't want to see how big the birch was.

She crossed the room to stand in front of me. My stomach now was one big knot, the smell of her flowery perfume making me feel sick.

'Left hand,' she instructed.

I held it out flat, thinking she'd go for the palm. That's what Mr Watkins at our primary school did, though his assistant Mr Crosby rapped your fingers with a metal ruler. Either way it was bad: I'd seen kids come back to class afterwards with their hands stuffed into their armpits, trying not to cry.

'Not like that.' Tutting, Mrs Emerson-Jones grabbed my hand, scrunching it into a fist.

I kept my eyes tightly shut. Halfway through a breath, the birch came down. She'd gone for the knuckles. The pain was white-hot. Like a burn. A sting. The worst of both at once. She did it again. And again. Then she stopped, and the pain got twenty times worse. She might as well have shoved my hand into a fire.

When I dared to look up, Mrs Emerson-Jones was back behind her desk again like nothing had happened.

The only sign was three white weals on the back of my hand. The pain made my eyes stream.

'Return to your lessons,' she instructed.

Yet as I turned to go there came the worst blow of all: 'Your parents will be informed of your poor conduct by afternoon post.'

The marks on my hand wouldn't be too hard to hide; a letter home was something else. Dad would have a flying fit. I'd be grounded. He'd stop my few pence pocket money. More than that, though, he'd be disappointed. The quiet girl with her nose in a book was fast becoming a bit of a rebel, and I didn't think he'd like her very much.

10

By the time I got in from school, Dad was waiting. He looked sad rather than angry, and for a moment I let myself hope that Mrs Emerson-Jones's letter hadn't arrived. Then I saw the envelope in his hand.

'Let's get this over with, shall we?' he said.

I sat down at the kitchen table. My dad stayed standing. He was in his shirtsleeves, coal smuts all up his arms. He'd been stoking the boiler, which never improved his temper. I wished Mum was home. She had a knack for taking the sting out of Dad, and she'd at least have asked how my hand was, and bathed it in a bit of warm water.

'Do you know what an embarrassment this is?' Dad held the letter in front of me. 'My own daughter fighting in school?'

He wasn't expecting me to answer, thankfully. It was easier just to stare at the salt pot.

'Why did you do it?' he asked, baffled. 'Was someone making fun of you?'

I shook my head. 'Not me, no. A friend.'

'So you thought you'd sort it out with your fists?' Dad asked.

'They were saying things about her colour!' I cried. 'It was horrible!'

'And your friend, what did she make of you wading in? Wouldn't she rather fight her own battles?'

I didn't know what he was getting at. 'She wasn't there.'

Dad took a deep breath, but if he was trying to calm down it didn't work. 'Do you know how hard we pushed for this place at St Kilda's? An opportunity like this – to better yourself by going to a good school – and what do you do? Throw it away!'

I flinched.

'Don't you know how important a good education will be? You're a girl, Lil, and a poor one at that. Life out there in the big wide world is going to be tough. All this talk of votes for women, equal rights. There's still a heck of a long way to go, you know.' He leaned in, hands flat on the table to stop them shaking.

'I'm sorry.'

'*Sorry?*' Dad fumed. 'You'll be sorry when you leave school with nothing, and watch all the jobs going to the local boys who've not an ounce of your brains!'

I was taken back. The last thing I'd expected was Dad to argue *for* girls' rights.

'One day, Lil, I want you not to have to live in a tiny flat and do a job that's god-awfully dull. I'd like you to go to university. I don't want you to be held back because you come from a working-class family or because you're a girl.'

I frowned. 'Me, go to university?'

'Maybe. Your grandad's not the only one who knows there's a world beyond London.' Looking suddenly tired, he straightened up, moving back from the table and reaching for his coat. 'You've had your punishment, and let that be a lesson to you. Your mother'll be home soon. You can tell her yourself what's happened. I'm going to the pub.'

I listened to him stomp all the way down the stairs and out into the street. In the quiet of our kitchen, my ears were ringing. I didn't know what to think of what Dad had just said, but I'd a strong feeling it wasn't a telling-off.

*

Only ten minutes or so later, Mum came hurtling through the door. She was red-faced, out of breath and holding her side like she'd been running.

'What's happened?' I asked warily.

'You've had … an invitation …' she gasped.

I stared at her. 'A *what*?'

'A lady … came into work …. Mrs Mendoza,' Mum puffed. 'Says you're friends with her daughter from school.'

'Mrs Mendoza came into *Woolworths*?' I sat forwards in my seat, sore hand forgotten. Now I was worried. Had something gone wrong at the last minute? Had Tulip's mum rumbled our plan?

'Don't look so horrified!' Mum smiled. 'She's asked to take you to Egypt, all expenses paid. It's a very important work trip, apparently, but her daughter's refusing to go without you.'

I was bewildered. What *was* Tulip playing at? I couldn't go to Egypt: I'd already told her so and explained why. It felt doubly cruel now that I was having to turn the offer down all over again.

'It's a shock to me too, Lil,' Mum admitted. 'I mean, we haven't even heard of this new friend of yours.'

'Sorry,' I muttered. 'Tulip's very kind to invite me, but I know I can't go. Dad won't want me to miss school.'

Mum wasn't listening. 'Wait there,' she said.

Moments later, she came back with her cardboard suitcase. 'They're catching the seven o'clock train from

St Pancras. Mrs Mendoza said to meet them there if you were coming.'

I couldn't believe what I was hearing. 'But Dad said—'

'And *I'm* saying,' Mum interrupted, 'that you'd better get packing if we're going to make the train. Come on, I'll help.'

I jumped to my feet before she could change her mind.

'Thank you!' I gasped, kissing her cheek. 'Oh, thank you!'

Rushing to my bedroom, I grabbed what clothes I could find. Not that I'd much to take – underwear, a couple of faded summer dresses, a sweater, my best blouse, a nightdress and a comb. I shook with excitement. It hadn't even begun to sink in that I was actually going to Egypt.

Yet when Mum laid the suitcase on the bed, and the lid sprang open, suddenly we were both staring at the slip of paper, and the word BOY in bold letters.

Everything went still.

I didn't know what to do, whether to close the lid or keep packing.

Mum moved first, smoothing her eyebrows with her fingertips, like she did when something was complicated.

'I should have left it somewhere less obvious, shouldn't I?' she said wearily.

'Is it yours – the label, I mean?' I asked.

She sighed. Nodded. 'You've seen it now. It's as good a time as any to tell you.'

Taking my arm gently, she made me sit on the edge of the bed, before perching beside me.

'Years ago, I had another child ...' She cleared her throat. 'I was only sixteen, and your dad and I couldn't afford to get married, so a nice family who couldn't have their own kiddies adopted him.'

But my mind was on Egypt and the journey I was about to make. I had that distant confused feeling Mum was talking to someone else.

A *brother*?

I looked at her in amazement. 'You had a baby?'

'That's about the size of it, love.' Mum got out a hankie to blow her nose.

I didn't know if I felt sorry for Mum or was fuming angry. Something had certainly stirred deep in my chest.

'But you gave him to someone else? Couldn't you keep him?'

Tears rolled down her face. 'That was the hardest part. We weren't married. It wasn't the done thing to have a baby like that – your grandmother was terrified I'd bring shame on the family.'

'And Grandad?' I wanted to know, because surely he wouldn't have cared what other people thought.

'He was in Egypt at the time. He didn't know about it until he came home, months afterwards. But we never forgot our baby, your dad and me.'

I didn't know what to say, or how to comfort Mum. But thinking of it now, I'd never seen my parents laugh much, or even look especially happy. Like most people did, I blamed the war, but maybe this baby they'd given up was part of it too. Maybe it was him Mum was thinking of in the evenings when she sat by the fire.

'What was he called?' I asked.

Mum sniffed, then smiled. 'Ezra, after his grandad. Every year on his birthday we go back to the convent where he was born. Just, you know, to say a little hello.'

'Which was why you went to St Mary's yesterday,' I said, because it was starting to make sense – or bits of it were.

Mum looked surprised. 'How d'you know that?'

'I thought you were taking Dad to see Grandad.'

'Fat chance of that happening!' Mum almost laughed, then looked teary again. 'Your dad thought it best not to tell you, but secrets have a sneaky way of coming out, don't they, eh?'

I felt too stunned to speak.

'We'd better hurry or we'll miss that train,' Mum said, smoothing down her skirt and getting up from the bed.

I didn't move.

'Come on, then!' Mum nudged me.

'I can't go. I can't leave you, not after what you've just told me,' I cried.

Mum took my face firmly in her hands. 'Now look here, Lil, this is too good an opportunity to miss. It's a once-in-a-lifetime trip. Think how incredible it's going to be! Your grandad would be so proud.'

'*Would?*' I looked at her. 'Don't you mean *will*?'

'Would ... will ...' She hesitated. 'I'll be truthful, he's not getting any better.'

Which gave me the last push I needed. I couldn't deny either the little anxious voice in my head telling me it was no coincidence that something so heart-wrenching had happened to Mum and Dad at the very time Grandad was in Egypt discovering ancient jars. 'Are you sure you don't mind me going?' I asked.

She nodded. She had tears in her eyes, and so did I.

'Just come home again, that's all I ask,' she said.

'I can't lose both of my babies, can I?'

I almost told her there and then about the jar, about Grandad and the curse, but it was a long old story and we really didn't have time.

11

For a wet Monday night, the traffic across London was heavy. We had to change buses twice, pulling up outside the station with only minutes to spare. I still couldn't quite believe this was happening, that I wasn't dreaming.

'Which train is it?' Mum was getting in a tizz. 'Which platform?' There didn't seem to be any guards to ask.

The station had the look of a place closing for the night. The tea stall was packing up, the flower seller sweeping the floor. At the ticket hatch the blinds were down. The only passengers seemed to be the ones making their way to the exit.

Then, the terrible truth.

On the far wall the huge station clock showed a couple of minutes past seven. We were too late. We stood, not speaking. I was dazed with disappointment. To have missed the train just by minutes was all too much.

Overhead, up in the rafters, a pigeon flapped awake. A hiss of steam came from a far corner of the station, and then the sharp, shrill unexpected blow of a whistle.

Mum and I locked eyes. 'Is that—?'

'Go!' Mum thrust the suitcase at me. 'You might just make it!'

The last I saw of her she was blowing me a kiss.

I ran full pelt across the station towards the noise. Behind a pillar, down a slipway and there was the sign: 'The Continental Express', though the platform was roped off in the way expensive paintings sometimes were in galleries. I slowed to a walk, excitement quickly turning to nerves.

What if Tulip had changed her mind? What if I couldn't find her amongst the passengers? What if I looked too poor to be allowed on board?

The train itself was lavender and cream-coloured, shining like water and fashionably curved. If Mrs Mendoza was catching a train it was definitely going to be this one. On the platform, whistle still in his mouth, was a guard in a uniform the same colours as the train. Despite giving my hair a quick smooth and rubbing my shoes on the backs of my socks, I felt myself growing shabbier by the second.

The whistle went again. The train was making ready

to leave. There were shouts, doors banging, steam swirling out from under the wheels. It was a job to see anything as I hovered at the barrier.

The guard came over but didn't unfasten the rope.

'You can't come through without a ticket,' he said, looking me up and down.

'I'm meeting some friends,' I protested. 'They're already on board. They've got my ticket.'

'Have they, indeed?' He might as well have told me to 'pull the other one'. It was clear he didn't believe a word.

Behind him another guard called out, 'Are we ready, Smith? All set?'

And then the clunk of a window sliding open as someone's head poked out. 'What's the hold-up?'

I knew that voice.

'Tulip!' I cried, waving wildly, then to the guard, 'There, look! That's my friend!' I'd never been so glad to see anyone.

Another dark curly head appeared beside hers. 'Bravo, Lil! You made it!' Oz yelled.

Even then I don't think the guard completely believed his eyes. But he unclipped the rope and seconds later I was running down the platform and boarding the train.

'Better late than never.' Tulip grinned, squeezing me into a hug.

On the platform, the guard's whistle blew again. This time, with all the doors shut, the train began to move. There was no going back. We were on our way to Egypt.

*

For the first few miles, we watched spellbound from the windows as the lights of London slipped away. I turned to Tulip. 'Your mother really hasn't guessed what we've done?'

'Not even a whiff of suspicion,' Tulip said proudly. 'She's holding court in the cocktail lounge as we speak. Already half the passengers are in love with her.'

This I could well imagine.

'You have got the jar, haven't you? And the translations?' I asked.

'It's all safely wrapped up in our room,' Tulip assured me.

'I'll tell Mama you're here,' Oz said and disappeared.

'Wait till you see where we're sleeping, Lil,' Tulip said, taking my hand. 'It's like a dolls' house bedroom – it's tiny.'

I felt a funny mix of nerves and excitement as she led me through carriage after train carriage. I'd thought the Mendozas' house grand, but this was swishness on another scale entirely. We went through a carriage done out with pale leather seats where people were smoking cigars, playing backgammon and cards. The dining car was quieter, full of rows of empty tables covered in white cloths as stiffly folded as envelopes. I couldn't help gawping at the curved wooden walls, the patterned ceiling, the thick salmon-pink carpets.

Narrow corridors linked the carriages together. With so many passengers milling about, we had to say countless 'excuse me's to squeeze past.

Finally we reached Carriage A. Oz's bedroom was next door, Tulip explained, and beyond that was the last compartment in the carriage, which was spacious, with its own bathroom, and had been nabbed by her mother. Ignoring the little ladder for reaching the top bunk, Tulip sprang up on to her bed. She sat there, looking down at me, swinging her legs. 'I've taken this bed. You don't mind, do you?'

'Course not.' I didn't mind a bit. The beds looked narrow but comfy with crisp turned-down sheets, and bars you could pull up to stop yourself falling out in the night. There wasn't room for much else – you could stand and stretch your arms out and touch both walls.

Reaching under her pillow, Tulip handed me something wrapped up in a sweater. 'You'd better have this back now you're here.'

It was the jar, in its box.

'I wasn't looking forward to sleeping with it later,' she admitted.

I wasn't entirely sure I was, either.

*

We found Mrs Mendoza in the dining car. She looked resplendent in a bright red frock and matching elbow-length gloves.

'Mama gathers new friends like flies,' Tulip whispered as we approached.

Mrs Mendoza, bright-eyed and smiling, was definitely a light-up-the-room type of person. I saw it, the other passengers saw it, and so – begrudgingly – did Tulip. I think secretly she adored her mum.

Once I'd said hello to Mrs Mendoza and, remembering my manners, said the 'thank-you-for-having-me' stuff, Oz, Tulip and me found ourselves a table near the window. Outside it was pitch dark, the rain streaking diagonally down the glass as we sped along. I still couldn't quite believe I was here, and wondered if back at home Dad had come back from the pub yet, if Mum had told him where I was. And like a wallop in the gut, it hit me all over again: I had a brother. He'd be a grown-up by now. He might've fought in the war. There was a chance he wasn't even alive, which was a crushingly awful thought.

'What's wrong with your hand, Lil?' Oz asked, getting my attention.

'What? Oh!' I flexed my fingers gingerly. The marks had gone from white to red, and felt tight like sunburn. 'It flipping hurt when she did it,' I confessed. 'But it's nothing a cold flannel won't put right.'

Tulip twigged what'd happened. 'You went to school today, and that old dragon hit you?'

'She hit me *three* times.'

Oz's eyes were on stalks. 'You got *caned*?'

'What on earth did you do wrong?' Tulip asked.

Quickly, I hid my hand under the table.

'Not much,' I said. 'Anyway, we're on an adventure. From this point on, all school talk is strictly banned.'

Tulip grinned. 'Sounds like my kind of rule.'

We shook on it.

Oz got to his feet. 'We should have a game of something. I'll find a chess set.'

As we waited for him to return, Tulip said she was hungry. Having missed supper completely, she ordered grilled cheese sandwiches, hot chocolate and a selection of fancy cakes.

'The *Washington Post* are paying, remember?' Tulip reminded me. 'They deserve it, overlooking Mama like that. Go on, order anything you want.'

I'd never ordered from a menu before. There was so much to choose from. I honestly wanted all of it, but settled on bacon and eggs, buttered muffins, and ice cream with fruit that came in a really tall glass.

'What's it like having a brother?' I asked as we waited for our food.

Tulip wrinkled her nose. 'They're loud, they're big, they're smelly. Everyone thinks they're more important than girls.'

'Not in your family,' I pointed out. 'Your mum treats you the same.'

'Maybe, but she still thinks I'm the giddy one, and Oz has got all the brains. It was the same with Alex.' She looked suddenly sad.

'We don't have to talk about brothers if you don't want to,' I said gently.

'*Half*-brother,' she corrected me. 'Mama's been married twice.'

I gasped. 'Crikey, like a movie star!'

'Her first husband was white, hence Alex not being dark like us. Our dad is black. He's a jazz pianist. Plays concerts all around the world.'

It sounded so very glamorous and intriguing.

'Everyone loved Alex.' Tulip sighed, fiddling with her napkin. 'The Golden Boy, we used to call him – and not just because of his hair. He was brilliant at everything.'

I remembered all the silver cups on the shelves in the Mendozas' library.

'He was going to university, to Oxford, to study Ancient History. When he came home from school in the holidays, he used to teach Oz. He said it helped him remember all he'd learned, going over it again like that.'

'But Oz must've been so young. How did he understand it?'

Tulip shrugged. 'He only picked up bits of it. The rest he's done since Alex disappeared – in his memory, I suppose. He's probably going to be as clever as Alex one day. It's the big wide world Oz doesn't understand so well. That's why he doesn't go to school any more.'

It was hard enough having a brother I'd never met, never mind how it must feel to have one and then lose him again. Mum and Dad in the churchyard yesterday flashed into my mind. It felt right, here with Tulip, to mention it.

'Apparently my mum had a baby before me.'

Tulip's eyebrows shot up. 'So now who's got the mysterious family, hey?'

'I didn't know him,' I said quickly. 'He was adopted years ago, before I was born. I've only just found out.'

'Gosh! That must've been a shock. Are you going to try and find him?'

'I don't think so.' It hadn't occurred to me to. 'Anyway, he'll be a grown-up by now, or I suppose he might be dead.'

We both fell glumly quiet.

Then Tulip slapped the table. 'Right, enough of this doom, gloom and misery. Where's our food and Oz with that chess set?'

Oz and the waiter arrived together. And soon our table was so crowded with food and plates and sparkling cutlery that it was a good job he hadn't found a chess set after all, as there was no space in which to play.

Tulip was relieved. 'Let's play something fun, instead. For matchsticks.'

She whipped out a pack of cards and spent the rest of the evening thrashing us both to smithereens.

12

Later that night, we caught the boat from Dover. The sway of the train became the swell of the sea as I crawled into bed, exhausted. At first light we docked in France and boarded another train that was to take us all the way to Athens. This leg of the journey lasted a whole three days, though unbelievably our new train was even fancier than the last. It had doorbell-type buttons in the walls you could press for tea and cake, and a seven-person orchestra that played all through dinner. Though my mind often drifted back to Grandad and the jar, keeping my spirits up wasn't too hard.

Very early on the second day, we passed through German forests, then the train started climbing into the mountains. The weather got much colder; ice formed on the windows, and we had to turn the heating in our cabin to 'high'. We went through tunnels cut into the mountainsides, and passed what to me looked like a frozen river but Oz insisted was a glacier.

By the end of the second day, we'd come through the mountains. The snow turned to rain and we dropped down in a dizzying fashion to the valley below. The fields and forests looked less green, and we started passing crops planted in long, low rows.

'Vineyards,' Oz said.

I caught Tulip's eye and smiled. She was right: her brother really was a walking encyclopaedia.

In the lull between afternoon tea and dinner that day, Tulip suggested we play a game.

'It'll be fun,' she promised.

We were in Oz's compartment. He was in his bunk, reading books that apparently had once been his brother's. Tulip and I were squished up on the floor. Sun was coming in through the window, and I could feel my eyelids getting heavier.

'Count me in,' I said, yawning.

Tulip asked Oz for his sketchbook, which he took from his bag and gave to her warily. With a sharp yank, she pulled out the middle pages, then laid them open on the floor.

'Pencil please,' she instructed. Oz passed her the one he often kept behind his ear. Then to me, 'Empty that glass of water, will you?'

She meant the one sloshing about on the night table. The only place to pour it was out of the window, which I did. Oz and I then watched over Tulip's shoulder as she wrote the letters of the alphabet in a circle on the paper. Oz guessed before I did what she was up to, which made me wonder if they'd played the game before.

'Ouija,' he muttered.

I knew the name – you pronounced it 'weee-geee'. Grandad said it was what the Victorians did in the days before radio sets, but Mum claimed it was just another way to tune in to different voices, and it depended on what you believed.

A chill lifted the hairs on my arms. It was probably too late to suggest a game of cards instead, and I didn't want to seem the scaredy-cat. If Oz was happy to play, I told myself, so was I.

'Close the blinds, please,' Tulip ordered. 'And the lamps – switch them off.'

She was bossy, I had to give her that.

The dark we'd created wasn't proper night-time black, but it was enough to change the mood. Tulip's next instruction was to lock the compartment door and pull the bolt at the top.

'We don't want any adults coming in and ruining it,'

she explained.

There was just enough space for us all to sit on the floor in a circle, though we had to draw our knees up to our chins and watch what we did with our elbows. Oz, I could tell, didn't like being so jammed in.

'Now join hands, everyone, and shut your eyes,' Tulip said.

Though I did as she asked, I'd a bad feeling this game wasn't going to be 'fun'.

'Spirits, we're here today to ask if there are any messages for us from the other side. Please, make yourselves known in a manner of your choosing.' Tulip's voice – heavy, slow – reminded me of school assemblies when the vicar read for hours.

Then my stomach made a slurping noise.

'Sssh, Lil!' Tulip tutted.

'Sorry!' I squirmed, half laughing, half horrified. 'I can't help it!'

Oz dropped my hand.

'Don't want to play,' he said. 'It's too much hand touching and being close.' He climbed back on to his bunk and promptly picked up his book.

'We'll do it with just the two of us, shall we?' I suggested.

Tulip shook her head. 'It won't work.'

But she let me take her hands, and when I shut my eyes again, she must've done the same, because moments later she was speaking in that same sermon-voice. I sat very still. Without Oz breathing next to me, it was easier to concentrate.

'Is anyone there?' Tulip asked. 'Give us a sign, spirits, if you can hear us.'

Nothing happened.

'Is there anyone there?' she asked again.

Behind me, the bunk creaked. It was Oz.

'You can't just call up any old ghost,' he pointed out. 'You need to have someone specific in mind.'

I opened one eye: Tulip didn't. Sitting ramrod-straight she told Oz, calmly and coldly, to shut up.

'So, spirit world,' she resumed. 'Do you have a male visitor for us, or is it female?'

Tulip dropped my hand, suddenly. I opened my eyes to see her finger now on the bottom of the upturned glass.

It began to move across the paper. It was obviously Tulip's doing, though that didn't stop it seeming eerie. The glass came to a halt next to the letter A.

'What's it saying?' Oz asked.

'A' was for Alex, of that I was pretty certain.

When Oz saw which letter it was, he sank back

on to the bed. 'I thought you said this would be fun, Tulip,' he said miserably. 'It's not real. You're making the glass move.'

'Shall we play something else?' I suggested, thinking this wasn't fair on Oz, who was clearly spooked.

But Tulip grabbed my hands. 'You try.'

I put my finger on the glass like she'd done. It didn't make any difference.

'Tulip, I think—' I stopped.

Something was happening. The room grew warmer, suddenly. I could smell dust.

'What's going on?' Tulip sounded nervous now.

The lamps, already switched off, flickered to life, then died again.

'I don't know,' I admitted.

Before our very eyes then, the glass moved. My finger was on it, but certainly not guiding it. It inched across the paper by itself.

Tulip got to her knees. 'Are you pushing it, Lil? You'd better not be!'

'No!' I took my hand away to prove it.

The glass kept moving in its funny, jerky way. It wasn't right, seeing a glass moving like that. The air around us seemed to fizz and prickle. I felt cold, and very afraid.

'You must've done something!' Tulip cried. She glared at me, at the glass, the paper, as if expecting to find a trick there.

'I haven't! I promise!'

Oz crouched next to me on the floor. 'That,' he gasped, staring at the glass, 'is incredible!'

I didn't think so. It felt wrong and creepy, though I couldn't look away as the glass moved clumsily towards the first letter.

Tulip willed the glass on in an almost-frenzy. 'Choose A for Alex!' It looked as if it might, then, at the last, it veered right and stopped at N.

'Write it down, somebody!' insisted Tulip.

Oz grabbed his sketchbook and pencil. The next letter came fast: O. Then a T, and a pause, followed by an H, an E, an R, another E.

I read the words aloud: 'NOT HERE.'

'What sort of message is that?' Tulip asked. 'And who's it for?'

I didn't know. But my heart was knocking so hard against my ribs, I wanted this stupid game to stop. The glass hadn't finished, though. The next word was IN. We looked at each other, still baffled.

'A person, maybe, or a place?' I caught myself thinking of the jar, and all the strangeness that came with it. Could the glass be trying to tell *me* something?

Hardly daring to breathe, I waited.

The glass didn't move. After a while, Tulip shifted to a more comfortable sitting position. Oz started twiddling his pencil. My mind, ever so slightly, began to drift. You could almost feel the mood in the room relax. All the signs were the message had ended.

Then, just as Tulip was about to speak, the glass shot across the paper. I jumped a mile. The glass spelled out the next word, then rolled on to the carpet, stopping against the sole of Tulip's shoe.

'NOT HERE IN AFTERLIFE,' Oz read from his notes. 'That's what the message says.'

Tulip frowned. 'What does *that* mean?'

'It could be about Kyky,' I suggested. Wasn't it why we were trying to return the jar, so the curse would stop and Kyky could finally complete his journey to the afterlife?

Or it could be about Alex.

'It's only a silly game,' Tulip reminded us, getting stiffly to her feet. 'Come on, we've been cooped up in here for too long.'

*

All that evening, Tulip kept gazing into the middle distance, or drifting off halfway through conversations. Oz, meanwhile, was tired and irritable.

'Whatever's the matter with you both?' Mrs Mendoza asked more than once.

In the end we went to bed early.

'The Ouija message bothered you, didn't it?' I asked Tulip when we were alone in our cabin.

She flopped down on to her pillow with a sigh. 'The way I see it is this: either I get my hopes up that Alex is still alive, or I ignore the message completely. Both things are heartbreaking.'

She had a point. But thinking about my brother – how odd to say that! – life had a way of springing things on you when you least expected them.

'Never say never,' I told her.

To my mind 'Not here in afterlife' had two meanings: a dead person stuck in limbo, or someone who wasn't dead at all.

13

At breakfast the next morning a strange telegram arrived. It was the latest from Mrs Mendoza's contact in Cairo, who kept her up to date on events in the Valley of the Kings. In the few days we'd been travelling, Mr Carter had been worryingly busy. He'd cleared sixteen sunken steps, at the bottom of which appeared to be a sealed-up doorway. Yet today's message had a rather queer ring to it.

'That poor canary,' was Mrs Mendoza's first reaction on reading the telegram.

We all stopped eating.

'Apparently Lady Evelyn – that's Lord Carnarvon's daughter – brought a canary to the dig so they could check there weren't any poisonous gases before going inside the tomb.'

'Did the bird die?' I asked.

'Apparently a snake killed it.' Mrs Mendoza tutted. 'Hardly thrilling, though, is it? How am I going to write a lead story about *that*?'

'What sort of snake was it?' Oz asked, looking up from his book. He never ate in front of other people, Tulip told me, yet he happily came to every meal just to sit there and read.

'Does that matter, darling?' But she read the message again, her finger trailing under the words. 'Bird bitten by cobra. Death almost instantaneous. Carter and Lady Evelyn trying to calm anxiety over possible curse.'

'Death shall come on swift wings,' Tulip reminded us. 'Looks like Mr Carter knows about the curse, but he's being block-headed and refusing to be scared off by it.'

More fool him, I thought grimly.

'Isn't the cobra a protector in Egyptian mythology?' I asked.

Oz nodded eagerly. 'Uraeus. The rearing cobra. Guardian of kings and queens.'

'Sounds to me like Tutankhamun's curse is trying to keep the archaeologists out,' said Tulip.

I hoped it succeeded, at least until we got there. Mrs Mendoza, though, looked positively cheered.

'You've given me a story, darlings, so thank you!' And she went off to type it up.

*

Later that day, the train made a stop at a little country station. Oz said it was in Yugoslavia, though I wasn't sure how he could tell. The platform was empty but for an old woman selling lemonade.

'Looks like someone's joining the train,' I said, pointing to a motorcar that pulled up just as we did.

Whilst Tulip and I were speculating on who was in the car – she thought a film star, I reckoned a spy – Oz announced he wanted some lemonade, so I said I'd fetch him one. By the time I'd done so, the motorcar had dropped its passenger and driven off. The man now on the platform was young, thin, not very remarkable-looking, so probably more a spy than a film star, I decided. Slopping lemonade, I hurried back to our part of the train. But not before the man called out to me: 'I say, where do I get on for second class?' because all of a sudden there wasn't a train guard in sight.

I pointed further down the train to the big '2nd' painted on the door, but he seemed a bit confused. He had two suitcases and a bag that kept slipping off his shoulder, and a not-quite-there-ness that reminded me of Dad.

Tulip was beckoning me furiously to hurry up. Thinking it the quickest way to get back on the train, I took the man to the second-class door, then hopped in behind him. Almost straight away, the train lurched forwards, and we were off.

'Thanks for your help,' the young man said, touching his hat brim. He had a straggly beard and a nasty scar under his eye. But his smile was a nice one.

Finally, a guard appeared, asking to see our tickets. I didn't have mine on me.

'Where's your destination, young miss?' the guard wanted to know.

'I'm going to Luxor,' I told him.

'*Are* you?' The young man perked up hearing this. 'Then I hope you'll be keeping an eye on Howard Carter.' Though he smiled as he said it, I'd heard enough about Mr Carter to detect an edge to his voice.

'I still need to see your ticket,' the guard interrupted. 'Who are you travelling with?'

'With Mrs Mendoza in first class,' I explained. 'And her children, Oz and Tulip. I can fetch my ticket if you like.'

The guard was actually quite jolly about it. The young man, though, who showed his ticket all fair and square, looked so very startled I felt sorry for him.

'Are you all right?' I asked him. 'Have you got on the wrong train or something?'

'What? No . . . no, I'm fine, thank you.' He smiled his nice smile. 'Keep an eye on Carter, though.'

'I will.'

And I gave him the lemonade because he looked in need of it.

*

Twenty hours later, we finally reached Athens. Just as we got off the train a new telegram arrived for Mrs Mendoza. My heart sank when I saw who'd sent it.

'It's from Mr Pemberton!' I whispered to Tulip. 'We've been rumbled!'

Tulip's mouth tightened – a sign she was annoyed.

'I don't believe this . . . *man*!' Mrs Mendoza cried, shaking the telegram in disgust.

'What's he saying?' Tulip asked.

'He's pretending I misunderstood him,' Mrs Mendoza exclaimed. 'Doesn't he remember the telegram he sent last week?'

'It's probably just a mix-up,' Tulip said quickly. I didn't know how she kept so calm when my insides were squeezing like a mangle.

Mrs Mendoza snorted: 'Well, he's ordering me back to London at once, the stupid fool. Says he's already sent a replacement man to report on the Carter story.'

I was horrified. We couldn't go back with our tails between our legs, not when we'd come all this way.

As we stood there, fretting, I caught sight of the second-class ticket man again. He almost looked like he was coming over to speak to us. Then Oz turned around, frowning, which seemed to put him off. He touched the brim of his hat before melting into the crowds.

'It really must be a mistake, Mama,' Tulip was still saying. 'All your tickets are booked, so someone at your newspaper obviously knew you were coming.'

'Let's keep going. We're only a boat ride away from Egypt,' I pleaded.

But it was Oz who said the exact right thing. 'And Mr Pemberton's sent another *man,* Mama.'

Mrs Mendoza straightened her shoulders. 'He can stuff his orders. We're not going to be beaten to the best story by some young pup, are we?'

I can't tell you how eagerly we agreed.

*

The telegram goaded Mrs Mendoza into action. Instead of stopping in Athens overnight we were now carrying straight on to Egypt. There were no more passenger sailings that day. But Mrs Mendoza refused to wait till the morning.

'I'm a reporter chasing a story!' she reminded us.

By the time we reached the port it was raining. A cold wind had picked up, and beyond the harbour walls the waves were white-topped and rather large for my liking. The English Channel had been relatively flat; just the look of the sea today was making me queasy. A few US dollars later and a man with an enormous moustache agreed to have us on his boat.

As soon as we got on board it was obvious we weren't the only cargo. From the hold of the ship came sounds of bleating. The smell was eye-wateringly bad.

'Ugh!' Tulip pinched her nose. 'What's that stench?'

'Goats,' Mrs Mendoza said cheerily.

I was, my stomach was beginning to tell me, not a very good sailor. But at least we were moving. At this rate – and if we got a decent connection in Cairo – we'd be in Luxor by Sunday. By my reckoning this was a whole day earlier than planned.

It was less smelly in the fresh air, so we stayed up on deck until the boat left the harbour. Surprisingly quickly, the coast of Greece shrank away behind us. What replaced it on all sides was the sea, as dark and steep as mountains. Though I clung on to the handrail for dear life, I'd soon had enough of being battered by spray.

'I'm going to lie down,' I told Tulip.

'I'll come too,' she agreed.

Our cabin was basic. The bunks were bare mattresses, the windows little misted-up portholes. But at least there was a slop bucket in the corner which, if my guts were anything to go by, I'd be acquainted with very soon. Oz was already here. He'd commandeered one of the bottom bunks by spreading out Alex's old Egyptian books, his own sketchbook, pencils, pens.

'How can you read in this weather?' I groaned.

'Easy,' he replied, without even looking up.

Outside it was getting stormier, and darker, and it was still only mid-afternoon. As Oz kept on reading, Tulip and I lay on our bunks, lolling this way and that with the waves. Every now and again there'd be a massive one that made your stomach drop like you were going over a bridge. All the while, I tried not to think about food, which for me was very unnatural.

When one particularly huge wave smacked into the side of the boat, it sent us and the cases sprawling across the floor. In a cabin so small there wasn't far to fall. But my suitcase came open – I already knew the catch on Mum's case wasn't the strongest. All my clothes scattered across the floor, Professor Hanawati's translations in amongst them. So too did the old cardigan I'd wrapped the jar in, but it unravelled somehow, and the jar was no longer inside.

Immediately I was on my knees, searching frantically through my clothes. Oz crouched beside me and peered under the bunk.

'It's here,' he said. Being smaller, he was able to slide his hand right in under the slats and pull it out again.

'Oh, thank you!' I took it from him. The jar was dustier than ever now, but luckily didn't seem damaged. Yet seeing it again – unwrapped, in daylight – made the back of my neck prickle. There was strange magic in this jar, all right. Tulip seemed to sense it too, for she started briskly rubbing her arms like she was cold.

There was something else not right with it: as I turned it in my hand it looked lopsided, like if you put it on a table it'd topple over. Worried that I'd damaged it, I held it to the light for a better look.

'It's the lid,' Tulip pointed. 'It's moved.'

She was right: the Anubis-head stopper was facing the wrong way. Anyone with eyes could see it had come loose. It didn't take much to open it, either, which was astonishing considering how before, when we'd heaved and pulled, it hadn't moved a jot. Now, all it took was a gentle twist, a dry, gritty grinding noise and the Anubis head was in my hand. The jar was open.

I glanced at Tulip, at Oz. In a flash, we were all peering inside.

'I can see something white,' Tulip said eagerly. 'Have a look, Lil.'

Slipping my hand in sideways, I touched what felt like very thick paper. Oh so carefully, heart in my mouth, I pulled out what looked like a scroll, neatly folded and tied with leather. I'd seen paper like this before in the British Museum: it was papyrus, made from a plant, Grandad told me, that grew in swamps near the Nile.

'Whoa!' Oz breathed in sharply. 'I bet that's *very* old!'

'What is it?' Tulip pressed. 'Can you open it?'

The papyrus looked so ancient it was almost flaking. I was pretty sure what it was, by now. It made it doubly exciting, and doubly important to see it all in one piece. Very gently, using just the tips of my fingers, I eased the scroll open a little way.

'I think it's Lysandra's account,' I told the others. 'The rest of it, I mean. Professor Hanawati mentioned he'd found it in the jar. Looks like he put it back there . . .'

Tulip whistled under her breath. 'Did he finish translating it?'

'I don't think so.' What I'd read only took us up to Maya choosing the tomb site. So if this was the whole account, the end of Kyky's story would be here too. The problem was, I wasn't an Egyptian scholar. Lysandra's tiny scrawl was visible through the paper, and backwards, forwards, upside down, I couldn't make head nor tail of it.

'I might be able to work some of it out,' Oz offered. 'With the help of these.' And he patted Alex's books, one by one, like talismans.

Dear Oz. His serious, big-eyed face gazing at the jar as if the secrets of the universe lurked there. Maybe they did. Maybe this was a chance for him to put into practice all the things his big brother had taught him, and he'd learned for himself. Or maybe it was simply the only choice we had.

'Do your best,' I said, handing the paper over.

Through the smeary porthole windows, late sunshine poured in. The storm outside seemed to be easing at last. Time passed. We lit lanterns and shared some biscuits. When Mrs Mendoza stuck her head round the door, we told her everything was fine.

*

It was morning before we knew it, and through the cabin porthole, Tulip announced, with a yawn, that she could see land. Together, we stood on tiptoe, staring at what almost looked like a line of cloud on the horizon.

'Is that really Egypt?' I asked.

Tulip smiled. 'Got to be.'

It was incredible to think we were nearly there.

'That's perfect timing.' A voice wafted up from the bottom bunk, making us both spin round. It was the first time in hours that Oz had uttered a single word.

'Did you manage to make sense of it?' I asked eagerly. 'Is it the ending?'

In answer, he patted places for us to sit not-quite-next to him, so we could hear the story he'd been poring over all night long.

LYSANDRA

Just when the gods seem to be smiling on us again, reports arrive of a battle in the north. Land that is ours has been seized by outsiders.

'We must teach them a lesson!' Horemheb roars from the palace steps. 'They cannot take what is not theirs!'

He asks for chariots, weapons, able fighting men.

There's tension in the streets, people are scared, but no one is ready to volunteer.

It's Kyky who suggests an alternative: invite the northern troublemakers to the palace for 'talks'. I'm astonished that Horemheb and Ay take him seriously. Yet, after much deliberation in secret, they do.

Households are asked to prepare food as if we're welcoming guests from afar. For the next few days we bake bread, make honey cakes. Our house is unbearably hot but smells delicious – good enough, I hope, to bring about peace.

The evening before the visitors arrive is moonless and mild. Just as Maya and I are readying for sleep, a familiar limping figure appears at our doorway.

'Lysandra!' Kyky hisses. 'I've had another dream.'

I beckon him inside. These days I'm wary of who might be listening.

'Was it the same again?' I ask.

'No.' Kyky rubs his temples like he has a headache. The old insect bite on his face is inflamed. 'There was a battle here, inside the palace. I had no weapons. I tried to fight people off with lamps, dishes, whatever I could find, but there was blood, Lysandra, so much blood.'

I fill with dread; this must be an omen for tomorrow.

'My only escape was through a door in the wall,' Kyky goes on. 'This time the door opened, and I was so glad, so relieved to walk straight through.'

I glance at Maya. He's gone pale. We both know what the open door means.

Kyky speaks first. He's shivering: 'I'm going to die tomorrow, aren't I? This visit is a trap. I should never have suggested it.'

Maya tries to comfort him. 'It might not be so.'

'Horemheb's lured the visitors here to kill them,' Kyky argues. 'He'll kill me too in the heat of the fight, then claim he was trying to defend me.'

I think of the broken chariot wheel, the whisperings at the window. People are plotting against our king, and have been for some time. Ay is impatient to take over as pharaoh. He cannot wait for his godson's life to take its natural course. I'm relieved Kyky believes us now, though it makes things far more dangerous. The scorpions and their poison are all around us.

'Dreams this vivid rarely lie,' I remind them both.

Kyky nods. He's terrified.

'If anyone attacks we fight back,' Maya says.

He's being serious, but the truth is my brother's no

warrior, and Kyky looks ill again. His injured leg still isn't sound, either. Against an army or an assassin, they don't stand a chance.

More importantly, I can't shake the dream. It's telling us Kyky will begin his journey to the afterlife tomorrow wherever he is, whatever he's doing. He might be murdered by his uncle's men. Or he might die peacefully in his sleep, or choke on his morning bread and honey. If it is to be his last day in this life, I believe he should spend it well.

'I've a different suggestion,' I tell Kyky. 'If you could do anything tomorrow, what would you wish for? Where would you want to be?'

Kyky and Maya look at me, surprised, as if ideas are their job, not mine.

Yet they understand what I'm saying and just before dawn they sneak off on foot, out into the desert, as far from the palace as the day's walk will take them. They'll throw fruit, hunt rodents, doze in the shade. They'll be their best and happiest selves. Meanwhile here within the city walls, I hope Horemheb and Ay's plans will fall as flat as a griddle on the fire.

The guests from the north arrive on horseback. As they ride up the main street towards the palace, we're meant to be welcoming them but instead, their strangeness makes us stare. The men are fair-haired, squat, ugly. Their horses look the same but with kinder eyes. Before they even dismount, Horemheb and his advisers appear on the palace steps, carrying swords. More of our men gather behind them, blocking the entrance to the palace. All are heavily armed. With a shudder, I think of Kyky's dream, and who this show of swords and daggers is really for.

Mother, like the others watching, is confused. 'Why aren't they letting them in? Did we not invite them here to make peace?'

I don't need to tell her. Word soon reaches us that the king is missing. He isn't here to receive his guests. The visitors are sent away, as confused as the townspeople, only with sorer tempers. From the palace, I hear shouting and the crashing of things being thrown across a room. As Mother and I go back to our chores, I pray that Maya and Kyky will stay away as long as they can.

Mid-morning, we're drawn from our work by a sudden darkening of the skies. The sandstorm is upon us in moments. Mother and I rush to bring pots, carpets, chickens inside, as gusts of wind tear through the courtyard. All along the central street, palm trees flail like horsewhips.

Once the shutters are closed at all the windows, Mother lights a lamp.

'It's a bad omen,' she says, shaking her head. 'Things have not gone well today.'

I'm nervous too as we wait out the storm, listening to the wind and the sand pelting our walls like a million tiny stones. My only hope is that Maya and Kyky have found shelter.

The storm, though fierce, blows over quickly. I'm anxious to know what's happening at the palace, so am glad to open the shutters again and have an excuse to be outside. Everything is coated in desert dust. There are drifts of it at our door, our gate. Servants are already clearing the palace steps, shaking out carpets and brushing down seats. Then one of them stops to stare into the distance. He points, says Maya's name.

I rush to the gate. They're back too early. The storm must have driven them home again. Yet the moment I catch sight of them it's clear something else is wrong. Maya is carrying Kyky over his shoulder, his head and arms lolling down my brother's back. He rushes *into the palace without a word. Fear makes me follow him inside.*

I find Maya in the main hall surrounded by men with swords. They won't let him pass.

'What's happening?' I cry. 'Let my brother inside at once!'

'Ay's orders,' one of the men says. 'We're not allowed to let anyone go beyond this point.'

'But you can see he's carrying the king! He's unwell! He needs tending!'

Maya tries to quieten me. The noise brings Ay out into the hall, where he observes the scene with dead-on-a-platter fish eyes.

'My godson has returned, I see,' he says, but when he realises Kyky's condition, there is no disguising his shock.

'Is he—?'

'Dying?' Maya interrupts. 'Yes. This time, I believe he is.'

We make Kyky as comfortable as we can. Medicines are sent for, bowls of cool water brought, but I don't think either will do much good. The bite on his face, the wound to his leg, both are red and blistering. I remember him last night rubbing his head, shivering.

He was falling ill even then.

'What happened?' I ask Maya.

My brother tells me how they'd travelled only a little way when Kyky asked to stop, the sweat running off him like rivers. He collapsed to the ground. Closed his eyes. He didn't get up again. No fruit was thrown, no rodents hunted.

'We'd already taken shelter when the sandstorm hit,' he explains.

All day Maya and I sit with Kyky. We try not to cry, try instead to count his slowing breaths and be thankful that he's been in our lives. When evening comes, as we light lamps and burn incense to cleanse the air, Kyky's breathing changes. His eyelids flutter. He opens his eyes.

I'm astounded. He's recovered! He's survived!

When I look at Maya he's laughing – laughing and crying at the same time. 'Are you staying in this life after all?' he asks.

Kyky gives a tiny shake of the head. 'No, but I don't want to leave you both. I'm scared.'

'The afterlife will be wonderful,' I tell him. 'Full of all the riches you could wish for.'

'Riches haven't brought me happiness,' Kyky says. 'All I want is to be with my friends.'

'Then don't die!' Maya insists, holding tightly on to Kyky's hand. 'What will I be without you? Who will I throw pomegranates at?'

'I can think of a few possibilities,' Kyky says, smiling.

He closes his eyes, then. A long, sighing breath leaves his chest. I sit silent, waiting for more, but no others follow. It's me who cries now. Maya gently slips his hand from Kyky's.

'Safe journey, my friend,' he says. 'I promise you this isn't the end, but a brilliant new beginning.'

The rituals start the next morning. Though sadness lies thick as smoke over the town, Kyky's body must be prepared for its glorious final journey, and it's a long, detailed task that will involve many. So often in Kyky's short life we've come close to this moment – fevers, accidents, a new limp, a different pain; it's hard to believe his time has finally come.

It helps us to be busy. Maya takes a bigger team of workmen back to the tomb site in the valley. They must carve rooms from the rock face, paint them, fill them with all the treasures our king needs for his new life. It's work that would normally take years, yet now has to be finished in just seventy days.

At the palace, Mother and I are summoned to wash

the body. Poor Kyky is a small, wasted figure, his arms and legs thinner than mine. With its old insect bites and new wounds his skin looks like a battlefield.

'He's still warm,' Mother comments, as we wash and shave his scalp.

'It's the fever,' I tell her. My hands, though, start shaking as I realise my terrible mistake.

My grandfather would never have made the error. He'd have listened to Kyky's dream, weighing it in his hands, and he'd have noticed the telltale signs of fever. His dream was confusing, bewildering, but it wasn't an omen – not a strong one. It was mostly nonsense, as fever dreams are.

My grandfather would have told Kyky to go home and take to his bed and rest. No doubt he would have advised an armed guard or two at his bedchamber door, but he'd never have sent him out into the desert where he thought he'd be safe, when he was hardly well enough to stand.

The mistake is mine. I am broken.

Other mistakes quickly follow. The tomb is in a difficult place. Fault lines in the rock mean it's dangerous to cut deeper into the hillside. Special equipment is needed, more plans, more workers, otherwise the whole mountainside will collapse. Ay tells Maya to choose another spot.

'But it has to be here, in this exact place,' Maya insists. 'I've measured the sun.'

Ay tells him there's no time for such details: burial rules state our pharaoh's tomb must be ready in seventy days. So it's no surprise when Ay takes over the plans. He chooses a new site at the base of the rock face. It's a shadowy, unlikely place for a royal tomb. Maya is furious: this alternative is a very poor second best. My brother wants to grab Ay by the throat and shake him. It takes all Mother's soothing to calm him down.

The preparations continue all day and into the next. Early in the morning, Ay corners me as I cross the courtyard. He reminds me of my duty as a scribe.

'These are important times, Lysandra,' he says. 'I'm relying on you to keep an account of all that is happening as we move from one king to the next.' This last he says with a proud tilt of the chin; I'm only glad Maya isn't here to see it.

Though my guilt over Kyky's death is strong, I hide it deeply. I find comfort in being busy, being involved. A priest is called to lead the embalming: I'm relieved it's his knife that cuts into Kyky's belly. We take the liver, lungs, stomach, intestines that he passes us. Their faint meaty smell makes me think of a butchered animal; this is no longer the Kyky I knew, which makes it a little easier. Mother and I, with a couple of the healing ladies, pack each organ in salt for drying. The same is done with the gaping hole in Kyky's torso. All that remains inside is his heart.

The priest is quick but careful. Inserting his hook up Kyky's nose, he teases out a grey shape with the look of fish gills. The brain is near complete, enough for Mother to scoop it up in her hands and place it in a basket on the floor. Later, we will burn it. Brains have no place in the afterlife.

Forty days pass. Forty soft spring days in which, as the grass plumps and the fruit trees bud, Kyky's body shrinks away. Ay becomes our new pharaoh: this is no surprise, either. Even Horemheb, who's always had the look of a leader-in-waiting, makes little fuss. It's Maya who concerns me. His anger is like a flame waiting to catch. Though I confess my mistake about Kyky's final dream, he refuses to think differently of Ay.

'That man has ice where his heart should be,' he says.

The tomb-building is not going well, either. The workmen Ay has hired are lazy and unskilled, their chisels making a mess of the walls that even last-minute plastering cannot disguise. The rooms are small, there are fewer than befit a royal tomb. When the sarcophagus is lowered in, ropes snap, a man's leg is crushed. The chamber that has been recently dug out is now full of rubble again, which only adds to the work. Night after night, Maya comes home cursing.

At the end of the forty days, we are ready to bind the body. At the palace, Mother and I take the organs from their salt, wrapping each in linen strips and packing them into the canopic jars.

When we uncover the body, something is amiss. The priest's knife wound has reopened. It's red and fresh. I'm startled. Mother tuts, says these things happen and not to make a fuss. We'll seal the wound with wax. But Kyky's left arm has also moved. Though we'd folded it across his body, it now lies at his side. The centre of his chest looks sunken. When I touch it, it feels hollow because there's nothing underneath.

'Mother,' I whisper in shock. 'His heart isn't here.'

She tuts again, reaches over the body to check it herself. 'It's no business of ours, Lysandra,' is all she says. 'Stop poking and pressing. We've work to do.'

But when she thinks I'm not looking she takes an amulet – a small one, shaped like the sun – and puts it in the place where his heart should be.

We wash the body, then rub it with scented oil. The eyelids and nostrils are plugged with resin-soaked fabric. All the time I'm thinking about Kyky's heart. Both Mother and I know it's not normal to remove it: a person needs their heart to live on in the afterlife. It's the centre of their being, what makes them who they are.

We put sawdust into his empty torso to give it shape, then just as Mother said, we seal the wound with wax. With prayers recited and incense burned, this alone is a whole day's work. Even by the end of it I'm still troubled by the missing heart. Someone close to the king has been meddling, taking what isn't theirs.

The next day we begin to wrap the body. We use linen strips around each finger, each toe. Occasionally between layers we stop to say a prayer to Amun or Osiris, or to tuck a lucky amulet between the folds to help Kyky on his journey. The process is meticulous. It takes days and days – fifteen in total. By the end of it our backs are ready to break, yet Kyky's form is strong and robust – far more than it ever was in life.

With the tomb as ready as it can be, the burial takes place. It's a bright, windy day as we walk the path down into the valley, the sounds of weeping women echoing off the rocks. Seventy days have passed, yet my guilt still hurts, and I miss our dear friend like a part of our family has gone. I'm no wiser about the whereabouts of his heart, either.

All through the ceremony, my brother is sullen, silent. The Opening of the Mouth ritual is performed by Ay himself. As he touches the place where Kyky's mouth is, I glance at Maya. My brother stays quiet. The air all around us is thick with things unsaid.

The first and second coffins are glorious and gold. Maybe Ay has done his godson proud, after all. Yet when the final lid is lowered on to the sarcophagus, it's clear it won't fit. There's an awkward, embarrassed pause. Ay starts blithering and blaming others. Maya thumps a wall, then storms out. I'm scared they'll go after him, but no one does. They're too concerned with the lid.

A workman is called. The outer coffin's feet are too big.

'Hack them off,' Ay says, bluntly.

The workman does as he's told, grunting over his saw until a pair of feet land on the floor with a clumsy thud. It makes me wince. The mistake is then hastily covered with stinking resin. It's an ugly business, hardly befitting a dog, never mind a pharaoh. In the tomb itself, the walls are covered with pictures – so crude and rushed the paint is still wet.

The ceremony continues. How jarring it is to be asking the gods to guide our pharaoh when a pair of feet sit before us on the ground. Finally, the prayers over, we file outside. I'm glad to be back in the sun.

Next, the tomb is filled with random objects: chariot wheels, baskets of linen, walking sticks, trumpets, fruit platters, oil jars, flowers tied in bunches. There are shabtis to guard the doors, swords, trunks. Apart from the sticks, I can't imagine Kyky needing any of this in the afterlife. None of it looks like items he once owned or was attached to. I'm wondering if Ay has simply cleared out an old back room at the palace and dumped its contents here.

High above us on the mountainside a white-clad figure catches my eye. Someone is up there, scrambling over the rocks. They're heading for the half-dug hole where Kyky was meant to lie. My mouth goes dry. It's Maya. I'm terrified he's going to jump or throw stones down on us in anger. He does neither: he disappears into the mountain.

It's then, like a lock unclicking, that I know what has happened to Kyky's heart. My brother has taken it. Without it our pharaoh is not complete, which means his journey to the afterlife won't be possible.

And this is Maya's plan.

He knows how Kyky longed to be an ordinary boy. The day he was made king was the unhappiest of his short life – that's what he told Maya. His true joy was in his friendships, not in the bitter wrangling of his own family, whose only interest in him was to further their own needs. To continue as a pharaoh in the afterlife would be torture for Kyky, not a reward. Perhaps this way, with his heart hidden inside the mountain, our dear friend will find some peace at last.

Wiping tears, I glance at Ay, fearful he's noticed what's happening above us. But he's still watching over the burial, swimming in his own glory. He thinks he's done well today, shown respect for the godson who in life he treated infernally. He will never read my account of Tutankhamun's last days. When he asks to see it, I'll lie and say it fell into the fire.

Meanwhile, if Maya's calculations are correct then on one treasured winter day each year the sun will align with Kyky's mountain resting place. I look at my brother, so thin, so awkward, and these days far too serious, and think of a saying Kyky's beloved grandmother used to use: 'The nut doesn't reveal the tree it contains.'

What it is, I think, is a saying about happiness. A nut that looks so dead and dry, given time, will grow into something lush, green and beautiful.

Rest assured, I won't be burning my account in any fire. I'll bury it in the same quiet place where Maya has laid our dearest friend to rest. Then, when my time comes – and Maya's too – we'll join him. And we'll be in the afterlife, all together.

PART FOUR

The youthful pharaoh was before us at last.

HOWARD CARTER, ARCHAEOLOGIST

14

Tulip was the first to speak. 'Cripes almighty! What Howard Carter would give to read all this!'

Never mind Howard Carter – I felt so giddy and shaken, I was glad to be sitting down.

'Kyky's heart *can't* have survived, can it?' I asked. It was mad to think it had. Yet hadn't Professor Hanawati mentioned something wrapped in linen, jammed in the bottom of the jar?

'Won't know until you look,' Tulip reasoned.

The very idea that a three-thousand-year-old heart was still inside the jar made me feel strange in a different way. To think that part of Kyky might be here with us – his blood, his cells.

I took a very deep breath. The jar lay between us on the bunk, the lid still off. I picked it up. Braced myself. As I slid my hand deep inside I half expected to touch something slippery and bloody – it wasn't, of course. It was dry, and came away fairly easily so what I now had in my hand was a piece of linen, neatly folded like a handkerchief.

'Open it!' Tulip urged.

I hesitated. The fabric looked frail.

'I don't think we should,' I said. 'What if it falls apart?'

Oz was sitting closer than usual. 'I'd really like to see it, Lil.'

Truth was, so would I.

'I'll do it slowly, then – and if it looks like it's going to crumble or tear, I'll stop, all right?'

The others nodded.

Ever so gently, I unfolded a corner. Then another. Amazingly, with care, the fabric stayed in one piece. As it came off, layer by tissue-thin layer, I began to feel something solid underneath. Much as I was desperate to see what, I was wary too. It felt wrong *and* wonderful to be poring over a dead person's heart. And all the time that familiar prickly, chilly sensation crept down my backbone.

'Careful!' Tulip whispered at my shoulder as I peeled back the final layer.

My breath stopped.

There was Kyky's heart, sitting in the palm of my hand, the size of a hen's egg. It looked like a clod of earth – flaky and mottled-brown – or the rusty tip of a centuries-old spear. You could almost see from the way it tapered at one end that it *was* the shape of a heart. It was incredible.

'Wow.' Tulip breathed. 'That's got to be the most astonishing thing I've ever seen.'

Oz shuffled even closer. 'I wonder, Lil, could I just—' He put his hand out to take the heart.

'No, Oz,' Tulip said. 'It's not respectful to pass it around. Let Lil put him back now we've all had a look.'

Gently rewrapping the heart one fragile layer at a time, I returned it to the jar and replaced the lid. Tulip, I realised, had just called the package '*him*'. This was what it had become: Kyky was someone we felt we almost knew.

Which brought me back to Grandad. Lysandra's descriptions of fevers and lungs and hacked-off feet were all reminders of the strange ways the curse was working. As soon as we got to Luxor, we had to find Kyky's burial spot. And be quick about it too. With that sense of foreboding still hanging over us, who knew when – and where – the curse would strike again?

'One treasured day each year ...' I murmured, going over Lysandra's words. 'If we knew what date, then we might be able to work it out from where the sun shines.'

Tulip shook her head. 'Too complicated. Anyway, calendars were different back then.'

'You're missing the point entirely!' Oz groaned, rolling his eyes. 'We're looking for a spot directly above where Mr Carter is digging. East-facing, high up in the rock face.'

He made it sound simple. And maybe it would be. We certainly had more details now than we'd had a few days ago.

'You're right, Oz,' I said. 'That's where we'll start.' Though the thought of searching in sight of Mr Carter made me more nervous than ever. I remembered the young man on the train who'd told me to keep an eye on him. Nobody, it seemed, quite trusted Mr Carter. The last thing we wanted was him getting his hands on the jar. He might not have thought much of it twenty-odd years ago, but if he knew what we knew now, well, he'd insist on examining it, putting it in a museum – or worse, taking it for himself. We could forget it going back to Maya's little tomb where it belonged.

Tulip tugged her bottom lip, staring thoughtfully at the jar. 'It's some story, isn't it?'

I nodded. It really was. Such a different story to the one the papers were telling, which was mostly all about Mr Carter. And that, I realised grimly, was another problem. For here we were on our way to Egypt with Mrs Mendoza, a newspaper writer in search of an exclusive.

'Tulip. Oz.' I looked them both in the eye. 'You're not to tell your mum about this, got it?'

Tulip nodded so fast I thought her head might bounce off. Oz, though, sat back, frowning.

'It's a decent bit of news,' he said.

It was, and I felt bad about it because I liked Mrs Mendoza very much. And it'd be a brilliant way to prove her priggish editor wrong. But we were here to return Kyky to a private, secret place, not blazon it all over the newspapers.

'In order to break the curse, we *have* to return the jar,' I reminded Oz. 'Don't think of it as Tutankhamun's heart – it's Kyky's, who never wanted to be famous in the first place.'

'But it's the sort of scoop that could make Mama's career, you know,' Oz pointed out.

'That's enough, Oz,' Tulip warned.

'She needs to find a big story,' he argued.

I took a long, slow breath. How could I explain I was doing this for my grandad, when all Oz wanted to do was help his mum?

It was Tulip who settled it.

'If you mention this to *anyone*, I swear I'll tell Mama—' She hesitated.

'Tell her what?' Oz challenged.

'Tell her who you thought you saw at Athens station!' Tulip blurted out.

I turned to Oz, intrigued. 'Who *did* you think you saw at Athens station, then?' because this was the first I'd heard of it.

He looked teary and angry. 'I'm not saying. You wouldn't believe me if I told you.'

*

An hour and a half later we docked at Alexandria. It was quite something to be standing on Egyptian soil at last: I could've sworn the soles of my feet actually *tingled*.

From Alexandria we caught a train to Cairo. I must've fallen asleep eventually because when I opened my eyes, it was daylight. Oz and Tulip were still asleep. Mrs Mendoza paused in her writing to point her pencil at the window.

'Look!' she whispered. 'Cairo!'

I sat up, rubbing my eyes.

We were coming into the city. The buildings near

the railway line were low, sand-coloured, packed tightly together. Between them were archways leading to little courtyards, alleys, roads, all busy with people going about their lives. I saw men in white robes, veiled women carrying pots on their heads. And rising above it all every now and then, I'd spot the dome or minarets of a mosque. Though it was still early morning, the light had a soft, peachy glow to it. This, I soon realised, was mostly dust, stirred up by carts, donkeys, motorcars and people walking. It was like the sort of haze you get at the start of a very hot summer's day.

I'd never seen anywhere so unlike the grey, wet London I'd left behind. The city was strange and beautiful. Everything I'd imagined it might be – and more. Through the little open vent at the top of the window I could *smell* Cairo: warm, dusty, animal dung, old apples.

I imagined Grandad all those years ago taking this same journey; he'd have been sitting here, just like me, not wanting to miss a second of it.

Before long, the train began to slow. Tulip yawned. Oz kicked out his legs and promptly woke up.

'We're here!' he cried, squinting at the window.

'Approaching Cairo station, yes,' Mrs Mendoza informed him.

The part of the city we were now passing through had streets as wide as London's, lined with tall, white, expensive-looking buldings. And like in London there were street sellers, newsboys, all shouting above the traffic. Then just before our train slid into the station itself, I caught sight of a horse lying in the road. It was still wearing its harness and looked rather dead.

'How awful!' Tulip covered her eyes.

'It happens in our country too, you know,' Oz remarked.

I'd never seen a dead horse in London. And the fact no one had moved this poor thing – carts, carriages, motorcars, donkeys simply carried on around it – reminded me, with a shivery thrill, how far I was from home.

15

Later that morning, we finally arrived in Luxor. The Winter Palace Hotel was a very fancy affair. It stood on the banks of the Nile like a giant frosted cake, with two sets of wide steps leading up to it, and a turning circle for cabs at the front. It was about as un-Grandad-like as any place could be.

'It's so swanky, Tulip!' I whispered, giving my dusty shoes a fierce wipe on the mat before going inside.

'It's *THE* hotel to be staying at,' Tulip whispered back.

Though she was clearly excited by this, it worried me. With a jar this valuable in my suitcase, experts and archaeologists were the very last type of people I wanted to be around.

'Is the Valley of the Kings far from here?' I asked.

'Only a few miles on the other side of the river.'

Which was better news. A quick wash and a rest in our room, and we'd sneak out when Mrs Mendoza was working. A few miles wasn't far: we could walk it.

Tulip was right about Mr Ibrahim: when I asked one of the hotel staff, he confirmed there was no one working here with that name. Not that we needed him now, thankfully. Lysandra had given us the details we'd been after.

Tulip was also right about the other hotel guests. The reception area was jam-packed with men in suits, and what with the bare marble floors and the ceilings full of whirling fans the place echoed like it did at our school pool on swimming gala day. Everyone seemed to be talking about one thing: the dig.

'... Carter's got till the Americans start complaining...'

'... the grave-robbers took all the gold ...'

'... there's something about that valley – gives me the heebie-jeebies ...'

As Mrs Mendoza fought her way to the reception desk, we waited with our luggage. It was hard not to be excited, but I was tired, which made everything seem loud and too bright. Poor Oz was also drooping badly, though Tulip had enough bounce for the three of us.

'Thrilling, isn't it?' Her eyes were everywhere. 'Can't see any women here, though.'

'There's one.' I nodded at a young woman who was sitting alone at a table. She had fashionably bobbed hair like Mrs Mendoza's.

Tulip gasped in delight. 'Do you know who that is?'

I shook my head.

'That's Lady Evelyn.' Tulip dropped her voice. 'Lord Carnarvon's daughter. She's the one who had the canary.'

Even before the canary incident, I'd read about her in the newspapers. Like her father, she collected old treasures and wasn't afraid of getting her hands dirty if it meant finding good pieces.

Standing here now, just feet away from such a key person in the Carter dig, didn't exactly steady my nerves.

Thankfully, at that moment Mrs Mendoza reappeared. Something was wrong. Fanning herself furiously with a piece of paper, she broke the news: 'Would you believe it, we can't stay here. Every single room is booked out.'

'No, Mama, that can't be right,' Tulip insisted.

I glared at her to shut up and not give the game away.

She mouthed back: '*I booked it, I swear!*' But at least she had the good sense to keep quiet.

'Oh,' Mrs Mendoza said, almost as an afterthought, 'this came for you, Lil.'

I looked down at the envelope she was handing me.

And there it was: a telegram from London. It was

signed by Mum, dated ten o'clock this morning. Nervous, I licked my lips. There was only one reason I could think of that my mum would send a telegram here: Grandad.

I didn't want to open it, but I couldn't bear not to. The others were discussing where to get rooms, so I turned away, just long enough to prise open the telegram.

'GRANDAD GLAD YOU'RE THERE – STOP – DOCTORS SAY FADING – STOP – SAYS GOODBYE.'

I didn't want to cry. Or collapse in a heap over this lovely marble floor. But right then I felt sure I was about to do both.

'What is it, Lil?' Tulip looked at me, concerned.

'It's not good news,' I admitted.

Tulip's face fell. 'Oh no! He hasn't—?'

'Not yet,' I said quickly before she could say the word. 'But he's going to, so we absolutely *have* to go to the valley today.'

She understood. 'Mama? Can we find somewhere, pronto, please? Lil and I are rather exhausted.'

'Mr Ahmed at reception knows a very nice place,' said a voice behind us. 'If you don't mind staying along the river a little way.'

We turned around.

Whilst all the other men were in jackets, the one now addressing us was in shirtsleeves, his arms nutbrown, his teeth large and white in his weathered face. I recognised him instantly in one big hotcold rush.

Howard Carter.

'Hullo, Madeleine!' he boomed. It took me a moment to realise he was talking to Mrs Mendoza. 'You don't have to tell me what brings you here!'

I felt my jaw drop – he *knew* Mrs Mendoza? She stretched out her arm. Most people I'd seen her do this to kissed her hand: Howard Carter shook it.

'You haven't enticed us all here for nothing, have you?' she teased. 'You have actually *found* something out in the desert?'

Instinctively, I slipped my fingers through my suitcase handle. I didn't dare look at Tulip or Oz. Nor could I believe their mother was on first-name terms with Howard Carter!

Mr Carter glanced over his shoulder, then leaned in. 'Oh yes. We've found something, all right.'

'Howard!' Lady Evelyn was on her feet. An older man who'd just joined her came over to us, holding out his hand.

'I don't believe we've met,' he said, greeting Mrs

Mendoza. 'Lord Carnarvon. A pleasure, I'm sure.'

I nudged Tulip: she nudged me back. Both of us stared at the small, slightly built man standing before us. His money was paying for the dig. His love of old artefacts had brought him all this way, which was funny, because he didn't seem that excited. If anything, he looked completely exhausted.

'Papa, we don't need to speak to *every* reporter crossing our path,' Lady Evelyn insisted, bringing a swift end to Lord Carnarvon's introduction before it had really got going. 'That new chap from the *Washington Post* hasn't even arrived yet and he's already cabled here, pestering for an interview.'

Mrs Mendoza's mouth hardened, just like Tulip's did when she was cross. True to his word, the editor's replacement was on his way. At least we'd got here first.

The conversation quickly changed tack, as if news reporters were something of a sore point. Lord Carnarvon, whose gracious smile was a match for Mrs Mendoza's, bid us farewell before disappearing off with his daughter.

'If you've nowhere else to stay, Madeleine, the offer's there,' Mr Carter said, all jovial again. 'It's a short way down the river. Mr Ahmed at reception will take you.'

*

The ferry took us back across the river. All the way, Mrs Mendoza gushed to Mr Ahmed about how grateful she was to him for finding us somewhere to stay.

'And,' Mr Ahmed told us proudly, 'it's very close to the Valley of the Kings, see?'

He pointed inland, away from the lush green riverbanks to where the landscape turned dusty and bare. In amongst it was a house where the motorcars parked outside glinted in the sun.

'How do you reach it?' I asked, trying to sound casual.

'Follow the path all the way past Castle Carter,' Mr Ahmed explained. 'On the main road, keep walking for two, maybe three miles. Valley is left of the road.'

I took careful note of all this, but had to ask: 'Castle Carter? Is that the house's name?'

'It's Mr Carter's home,' Mr Ahmed said. 'See how close he lives to where you'll be staying! How wonderful for you!'

'He's keeping an eye on us,' I muttered under my breath, as we lagged behind the grown-ups. 'That's why he recommended it.'

'Then we'll keep an eye on him too, won't we?' Tulip insisted.

Which was exactly what the young man on the train had said. I also kept in mind Grandad's point about how Mr Carter dazzled people like a sun king. Yet not everyone was suspicious of him. It seemed he'd already cast his spell on Mr Ahmed.

On the other side of the river, we had to go along the bank, past fishermen and boat-menders, with stray dogs sniffing at our heels. We were walking for what felt like ages. It was awfully hot. On a day like this in London we'd be sitting in the park, eating ices. Here, the local men wore their *galabiya* – the long shirt-like gowns – with jackets over the top, jumpers, knitted waistcoats. A few had on hats and scarves.

'An Egyptian winter,' Tulip said, lifting her hair off the back of her neck. 'Imagine what it's like in summer.'

We passed a boy about our age, barefoot in a *galabiya*, with a huge, woolly scarf around his throat. He was tending a pair of grumpy-looking camels; when he saw us he beamed, and despite how grim I felt, I managed a smile back.

'Don't encourage him!' Tulip warned. 'He'll think you want to buy his camels.'

'Are the camels for sale, then?' Oz asked.

'They could be for hire.' I pointed to the squares of carpet on their humps. On top of each was a wooden rack that might've been for clinging on to: I couldn't imagine how you'd actually sit on it.

Tulip fell about laughing at the camel nearest us. 'Ha! That one looks like you, Oz!'

Oz didn't see the funny side.

*

Shortly after the camels, the path got fainter, the palm trees thicker. My feet were dragging. Much more of this walking and we'd be back in Cairo again. At last, up ahead, I saw a jetty where a boat was moored, the sort of boat people lived on. Like a barge.

'*Dahabiyeh*.' Mr Ahmed gestured to the boat. 'Yours, my friends, for as long as you wish.'

I gasped out loud: I couldn't help it, because it was, without doubt, a splendid place to stay. The boat was long and low in the water, with a beautiful white balcony that gleamed in the sun. On deck there were hammocks and armchairs for lounging in, and from inside came herby, meaty smells of something delicious being cooked.

'I expect Lil's had enough of boats, haven't you?' Tulip grinned, reminding me of what a lousy sailor I'd been on the journey from Athens.

'I love it,' I admitted, and from the glint in her eye I knew she did too.

It struck me again how clever she was – not bookishly like Oz, or Alex, but in how she reached out to people. I'd needed her help and she'd given it in spade-loads. She'd booked our train tickets, *tried* to get the best hotel rooms – all without batting an eyelid. But for her, and her family, I'd still be in London, waiting for Grandad to die. At least here we had a fighting chance.

'Thanks, Tulip,' I said. 'For everything.'

She looked at me with that confident, lopsided smile I'd come to love. 'Don't thank me yet. There's plenty that still could go wrong.'

She was right about that too, as it turned out.

16

If I'd had my way, I'd have set off into the desert the moment we'd put down our bags. But the others were tired – we all were – so I agreed reluctantly to at least have something to eat. It was early afternoon by now. The heat up on deck was bearable as we sat on giant cushions, eating fish wrapped in bread. It was served with tomatoes and red onions and something that looked like parsley but tasted soapy, and was absolutely delicious.

All the while, I kept an eye on Mrs Mendoza. She was bound to disappear sooner or later to write. And when she did, we'd be able to sneak off to the Valley of the Kings. At least, that was the plan.

Instead, I fell asleep. When I woke up it was mid-afternoon. I scrambled to my feet, dry-mouthed and bleary-eyed.

'Why didn't you wake me?' I said to Tulip, who was lounging nearby with her feet up, drinking iced tea.

I was annoyed we'd wasted so much time.

'You needed the rest,' she replied.

Mrs Mendoza was nowhere to be seen.

'Mama's gone to a cocktail party tonight at the hotel,' Tulip told me.

'In which case . . .' I caught her eye.

Tulip nodded. She drained the rest of her drink. It was time to go.

Down in the cabin I was sharing with Tulip, I rummaged through my unpacked suitcase for my satchel and the jar, trying not to dwell on how nervous I was. Back up on deck, Oz was settling down in a hammock with an armful of books. I felt guilty for shattering his peace.

'What, *now*?' Oz huffed a bit when I told him we were going straight away.

'Yes, *now*!' Tulip replied irritably.

'If we go now there might still be a bit of daylight left.' I said. 'Especially as we don't completely know the way.'

'And we've got to climb a rock face when we get there,' Tulip added with a grimace.

I squeezed her shoulder; I wasn't looking forward to that part, either.

*

The walk wasn't particularly difficult at first. It'd got cooler in the last hour or so, and the path which Mr Ahmed had shown us was flat and well marked. Though deep down I was tired out, I couldn't have rested even if I'd wanted to: Mum's telegram had put paid to that.

Leading us away from the river, the path dropped between two stone walls, then, as the ground rose up again, Castle Carter came into full view. The house looked formidable, square and stern. All the blinds were down at the windows, though someone was obviously at home because you could hear jazz playing on a gramophone. The motorcars were still parked outside.

'There's something about that man,' Tulip said, wrinkling her nose. 'I don't trust him.'

'Me neither,' I agreed.

A few hundred yards beyond Castle Carter we came to the main road. It was busy with motorcars, carts, camels, all churning up dust.

'Two miles this way, I think,' I said, pointing ahead.

In fact, we'd only gone about a mile when to our left, the road suddenly dipped.

And there, laid out before us like a painting on a wall was the most spectacular view. The whole valley was bare rock. No trees, no grass, not even a bush. Everything was the same pale, golden colour, stretching on for as far as you could see under the setting sun.

Oz, who'd been looking rather droopy, sprang to life. 'I should've brought my sketchbook! I want to draw it – all of it! From every angle!'

'And you can,' Tulip reassured him. 'Later.'

'Down there, look.' I pointed to where the road disappeared round a rock that jutted out. 'I bet that's where the Carter dig is.' There wasn't an actual opening to see – just a few white tents pitched up, some tethered donkeys, local men carrying baskets on their heads. There were power cables running across the dirt. A man was taking photographs, though the young boys carrying water kept getting in the way.

'I can't believe this is actually it!' Oz gasped. 'The Valley of the Kings!'

Bizarrely, I *could* believe it. I felt it too. That strange sense of dread had come over me again, and a chill slithered down my neck.

'I wouldn't want to be buried here,' Tulip said.

I knew what she meant: there was so much rock, so much sky, that the whole valley made you feel tiny in a way that was almost menacing. It was the sort of place you'd perish in, if you weren't already dead. And somewhere in it, away from all the fuss, the water boys, the electric cables, was the place where Maya meant his best friend to lie at peace.

The next big question for us was how to find it – and to do so without Howard Carter noticing. If we stuck to this side of the valley, we'd at least stay out of sight as we descended. Not that there was a path, as such. From up here the hillside looked alarmingly steep. And there was a general feeling that I'd be the one to lead the way. 'Go slowly,' I called over my shoulder as I took my first steps. 'Don't look down, either,' I added, as a quick glance at the valley floor made my head swim.

Once we'd got going, it wasn't too bad. We were almost a quarter of the way down the hillside when I heard Oz call out behind me. I turned around to see him pointing at the sky.

Something had happened to the sky. One moment it was low and red, the next it dimmed like it had gone behind a cloud. Only there were no clouds, just a huge, billowing wall of dust coming towards us at alarming speed. Within seconds we were in the middle of a yellow fog. It wasn't like a London pea-souper: it was hot and gritty. It made my eyes sting, my mouth go powder-dry. Now I really couldn't see anything but swirling, churning sand. We froze on the hillside. One wrong move might send any one of us plummeting to the valley floor.

'Yikes, this is horrible!' Tulip yelled. I was so glad to hear her voice. Even more glad when I felt an arm, then another arm, and Tulip wrapped herself tightly around me, burying her face between my shoulder blades.

'Oz!' I cried. 'Are you there?' I didn't hear him reply.

'We'll have to sit it out,' I said, praying that Oz was nearby too, and being sensible. I'd read about sandstorms but that didn't prepare me for what it was like to suddenly be in the middle of one. The whole sky had gone thunderstorm-dark. The wind picked up too, whipping around our heads, blowing sand everywhere. I clamped my hands over my mouth. Shut my eyes. Behind me, Tulip groaned. 'It's vile!'

'Stop talking!' I told her.

I'd no idea how close we were to the edge of the hillside. There was nothing to cling on to. Everywhere was sand. It was in the air. On the ground. In my ears, up my nose, crunching between my teeth. Even when I did open my eyes just a sliver, I couldn't see further than my hand.

I'd an eerie feeling that this sandstorm wasn't a coincidence. Perhaps they were common in these parts; I didn't think so, somehow. A sandstorm had happened on the day Kyky died. A young man, caught out in bad weather, had perished.

I stood bolt upright, frantic: 'Oz? Where are you? Answer me if you can hear me!'

From somewhere above us came a little bleat of a cry. Tulip was on her feet now as well.

'Hang on! We're coming!' I yelled. My heart was thumping. I couldn't breathe or find my bearings. All I knew was Oz was on his own on the hillside, and we had to get to him.

'Just stay where you are!' Tulip shrieked.

Whether he heard, I'd no idea. Wind and sand kept swirling around us. I inched along, half a step at a time, terrified of being too close to the edge of the hill. Tulip crouched behind me. I had to trust the ground beneath my feet. Oz must be nearby. And when I saw a glimmer of blue sky, and the wind began to drop, I almost started to run.

If I had I'd have gone slap-bang into him – not Oz, who was sitting quite sensibly on the ground, looking dusty but unharmed, but the back of someone wearing a grey-striped *galabiya*.

The man was shouting and waving his arms. 'You're crazy to try and walk in a storm! What were you thinking?'

Tulip rushed over to Oz, which left me facing the arm-waving man. As the storm quickly cleared, I saw it wasn't a man, but the boy from earlier who'd had the camels, and who definitely wasn't smiling now.

'It's not like walking on your English beaches!' he yelled at all of us. 'You have to know the sky, know the signs. The valley is a strange and moody place. It's dangerous for people who don't understand it!'

I felt a bit embarrassed.

'Thanks for finding Oz. We're really grateful,' I said.

Tulip, all smiles now, tried to shake the boy's hand but he backed away. 'You English, you come to our country with your cars and your electric cables and think you can triumph over anything! It's not like that out here – it's a different sort of place that requires respect and patience!'

By now, I was starting to wonder if Mr Carter was at the root of his anger. And when Tulip asked, ever so sweetly, for directions down into the valley, that seemed to firm up the boy's view that we English were in this together.

He gave us directions, all right. Long, complicated

ones that led us uphill and downhill until eventually we were back by the river where we'd started. The boy had sent us deliberately the wrong way. It was so exasperating. It was almost completely dark.

'What do we do now?' Tulip asked, looking pretty fed up.

I shook the last of the sand from my hair and shifted my satchel on to the other shoulder.

'We head straight for the Carter site and climb upwards,' I said. 'The plan hasn't changed.'

Tulip nodded. 'You're right. We've got to try again.'

Oz didn't say anything. But he was the first of us to turn on his heel and set off in the direction of the desert.

17

I'd never expected an Egyptian evening to be so cool. Under a clear, starry sky with mist coming off the river, it could almost have been England. Yet it wasn't England: the hum of insects and the smell – like dust and sweat and mint all mixed together – told me exactly where I was. I felt excited again. Terrified. I sensed it in the others too: Tulip was unusually quiet; Oz, up ahead, was whistling under his breath.

This time, as we passed Castle Carter, there was a single light on at a downstairs window. The cars that'd been there earlier had gone.

'I expect he's at the cocktail party,' I reasoned.

Still, we hurried past and had almost reached the main road when Tulip, who was bringing up the rear, suddenly yelped.

'Arggggh! Something's bitten me!'

In the dark, I could just about see her holding her foot and grimacing. Very gently, I helped her sit down.

'Is it bleeding?' I crouched beside her.

'Don't think so.' She gritted her teeth to check. 'Arrrggh!'

'Did you see what did it?' Oz wanted to know. 'Was it a snake, or a dog?'

I didn't like the idea of either.

'We'd better have a look at the bite,' I said.

As Oz flicked on his torch Tulip, begrudgingly, pulled down her sock. You could see a bright red mark just below her ankle, though thankfully no blood.

'It really flipping hurts!' Tulip gasped.

'Can you get up?' I asked.

'I think so.'

But once she was on her feet, she couldn't walk more than a few steps. The pain made her catch her breath. I felt suddenly close to tears.

'No crying,' Tulip said sternly. 'I'll be fine in a minute.'

But it was obvious she wasn't going to manage a two-mile trek in the dark, then climb a cliff face at the end of it. We had to take her back to the boat and fetch Mrs Mendoza – and probably a doctor too.

'Oh no,' she insisted. 'I'm coming with you, even if I have to crawl on my hands and knees.'

'But we don't know what's bitten you. It could be

poisonous.' All sorts of things like rattlesnakes and deadly spiders lived in desert places: if she'd been got by one of those we were in trouble.

Tulip was stubborn. 'I mean it, Lil. After all we've been through to get here, I'm not dropping out over a stupid bite.'

'It looks like a sting,' Oz pointed out.

We didn't know for sure, though, did we? If someone could just look at it and tell us . . .

'We'll have to carry her back.' Oz interrupted my thinking.

Tulip snorted. 'Lil's not a beast of burden!'

I wasn't, but it did give me an idea.

*

The boy with the camels was easy enough to find. It was his animals I saw first, dozing in the grass. On seeing me, one of them grunted. The other chewed and stared, then spat on the ground. It wasn't much of a welcome, but after earlier, I wasn't expecting one.

The boy himself was crouched on the riverbank, cooking eggs over a fire.

'Hello,' I panted, out of breath from running. 'I'm afraid I'm here to ask for your help again.'

The boy prodded his eggs till they spat aggressively in the pan. I supposed he was still angry at us for needing rescuing earlier.

'I'm sorry about the sandstorm business.' I tried to be polite like Tulip. 'But my friend's been bitten by something and I hoped you might be able to help?'

The boy stood up, taking his pan off the fire. He was still wearing his enormous scarf, which made his face look small and sharp, his eyes bright.

'It is not only the sandstorm I am angry about,' he said. 'Earlier today when you passed on the riverbank, you were most rude.'

Thinking he meant Tulip's comment about the camel looking like Oz, I tried to explain. 'My friend made a joke, that's all. We weren't laughing at you.' But hearing how shoddy it sounded, I felt myself go red all the same.

'Let's do things properly this time, shall we?' The boy wiped his hands, then offered me one. 'I am Pepe. My camels are called Charlie and Chaplin after the famous movie star.'

'I'm Lil,' I stuttered, shaking his hand. 'Your camels have excellent names!'

Pepe didn't smile. 'We are honest and have feelings, and offer a very good service to tourists like you. If you and your friends only want to laugh at us, find yourselves an old mule too deaf to hear.'

'I'm very sorry, Pepe,' I was starting to get flustered. My apology wasn't working and I was desperately worried about Tulip. 'We didn't mean to upset you, or your camels. But my friends, Oz and Tulip, are really nice people, and we're trying to do something terribly important tonight and—'

Pepe held up his hand to stop me. 'No speeches, please. Show me to your friend.'

*

Pepe insisted on bringing the camels in case Tulip couldn't walk.

'I'm absolutely *not* getting up on one of those!' she cried, when she saw Chaplin and Charlie. 'I can manage, thank you.'

She couldn't, of course. And it was Pepe's turn to laugh when Tulip had to give up after a few steps.

'Please, Tulip,' I begged. 'Just let Pepe look at your bite.'

Rolling her eyes like I was making a huge fuss, she pulled down her sock for him to see. The wound definitely looked worse. It was red and swollen, about the size of a hockey ball, with two marks in the middle where the skin was pierced.

'How bad is the pain?' Pepe asked.

Tulip grimaced. 'Like red-hot worms crawling up my leg.'

It sounded awful.

Pepe sat back on his heels. 'Ah, that will be a scorpion.'

'Crikey! I've never seen a proper scorpion sting before!' Oz said with relish.

Tulip looked at me, terrified. I held her hand.

'No, no,' Pepe reassured us. 'A scorpion sting is good – at least, it's better than a snakebite. You won't die.'

Tulip tried to joke: 'Well, that's one less thing to worry about.'

But it wasn't, was it?

In a whirl of panic, I remembered Kyky's dream: scorpions were in it, crawling over his feet. It was another bad omen, Lysandra had said. A sign of danger. Death. Poison.

I told the others as quickly and as plainly as I could. If, as I'd been dreading, the curse was now stalking us, then Tulip was the next victim. None of us was immune.

'Then we absolutely can't delay any longer,' she said, squeezing my hand tightly.

'Where is it you are wanting to go?' Pepe asked.

When I told him, he looked at me like I was mad. 'To the pharaoh's tomb, *tonight*?'

'Not the pharaoh's tomb exactly – the cliff above it, to be precise, and quickly too, if you don't mind.'

He shook his head. 'Oh no. No one goes there at night.'

My skin prickled. The valley had a strange, eerie feel to it, all right – I'd sensed it myself – but we were well beyond being put off by it.

Though Pepe meant something else. 'There are special rules for visiting the valley these days.'

I frowned. '*Rules?*'

'Oh yes, thanks to your *Mr Carter* we can't even walk in our own desert without a permit, an Egyptian official and plenty of this.' Pepe rubbed his fingers to mean money.

I wanted to point out he wasn't *my* Mr Carter, but I understood.

'We have to go there,' I begged. 'It's for my grandfather. We've come all this way to do this one thing just for him.'

Pepe breathed in through his nose, considering it.

'Will Tulip be all right?' I asked.

'It's a risky trip for everyone,' he said. 'But as you've asked politely and it's for your family, I am willing to overlook two of these requirements.'

*

It was a relief to get going at last. A mere click of Pepe's tongue and the camels lay down – all spindly legs and knobbly knees, and so awkward they looked more like folding tables than animals.

'Charlie is the sensible one,' Pepe explained.

'I'll have him,' Oz said, and before anyone could argue, he'd scrambled on board.

'And Chaplin here is the show-off,' Pepe told us, though both camels looked the same to me.

I was right about the saddles. They were horribly uncomfortable and scratchy against your knees. And when our camel knelt on his front legs to stand up, I was petrified we'd slide down its neck. At least with two of us – me in front, Tulip behind – it meant we were wedged in tight.

The actual 'riding' part wasn't too bad, either, like sitting in a bony armchair. The miles went by quickly. As it was late, there was no traffic on the main road.

It was dark as anything, which meant it wasn't hard to think of curses in a place like this, or of ancient magic taking its revenge. When I felt myself getting scared, I thought of Grandad and patted my satchel for reassurance. And when I wasn't worrying about him, I kept asking Tulip if she was all right.

'My leg's going sort of tingly and numb,' she said. 'It feels weird, but it's better than the pain.'

Pepe's way down into the valley was quicker, and steeper, than ours. It wasn't the easiest route, he explained, but it was the most secret.

'There are guards patrolling,' he told us. 'They'll arrest us if we're caught without the proper papers, I warn you now.'

As soon as we left the road the darkness changed. It got thicker. Colder. Under Pepe's firm orders we kept absolutely quiet.

'All you must do is hold on tight,' he instructed. 'Trust your camel: he'll know where he's going.'

I wasn't sure how true this was, because at first Chaplin kept stumbling over every rock we came to. I felt mean not turning my torch on to help him, but Pepe laughed quietly. 'You think camels use torches? They see by starlight.'

I looked up when he said that – properly looked up,

I mean, until my eyes got used to the night.

'Oh, Tulip,' I whispered. 'Have you seen the sky?'

She hugged me a little tighter round the waist. 'Dear Lil, I've been looking up at it for miles.'

In London, you only saw the faintest stars right in the middle of the sky. Here they were everywhere, right down to the far-flung corners and all along the edges. There were almost too many, if that were possible.

What I saw now, over to our left, looked like yet another one. Except stars didn't move from side to side.

Oz had seen it too, and turned in his saddle. 'Pepe, what's that over there?'

The light was below us on the path, and as much as I could tell, not that far away. It stood out quite clearly, bobbing a little as it moved. We all stopped to watch.

'It's coming from the tomb site,' Pepe explained. 'It appears to be a torch.'

The camels began to plod forwards again, the path levelling out as we reached the valley floor. Over to our left, the torch beam kept moving. Someone else was very definitely there.

'You have to have a permit to be in the valley,' Pepe reminded me. 'And the company of an Egyptian official. It is the law, even for Mr Carter.'

A law we were breaking, I thought nervously: we didn't have a permit, and surely Pepe wasn't old enough to be an official.

'Who d'you think it is, then?' I asked.

'Only the guards. *Probably*.'

18

Half a second later we were lying flat on the ground, even the camels. Something large and white loomed in front of us – a canvas tent. My heart was going like mad, and I'd a mouthful of dust, but when I heard voices I realised just how close to Carter's site we were. In fact, we were *in* it, exactly as we'd wanted to be. Only it suddenly didn't seem like such a great idea.

'Pah! As I suspected – guards!' Pepe muttered in disgust.

Tulip groaned. 'Just what we need.'

Propping myself up on my elbows, I peered around the tent. The torch had gone out. The voices had stopped too. I didn't dare move an inch more, in case the people were still there.

Oz wriggled alongside me. 'Torch batteries aren't very reliable. Though it depends on the type—'

'For crying out loud, shut *up*!' Tulip hissed violently.

'Easy, Tulip!' I whispered.

Oz sniffed. 'You never listen to me. Not about torches, or the man at the station.'

Why was he on about that again? The only man at the station I could think of was the one with the nice smile who'd told me to keep an eye on Mr Carter. What it meant to Oz I didn't know, but he was awfully upset about it. And when I tried to touch his arm, he turned his back on me.

'It's this valley.' Pepe shivered. 'It casts bad spells on people. Makes them argue and fight.'

Like Grandad and Professor Hanawati, I thought grimly, who'd come here and never been friends again.

We fell into a tense silence. Without the torchlight flitting around it was easier to see things. Just in front of the tent was a heap of rocks, a wheelbarrow, what looked like the electric cables we'd seen earlier running past us in the sand. Beyond that, I saw hooves and swishing tails. Four donkeys were tethered, nosing through a pile of dry grass that'd been left for them.

Beyond it, the sides of the valley rose almost straight up. My stomach fluttered. Somehow, we had to climb that rock face without being seen. Shifting my satchel to the side, I got into a crouching position: 'I'm going to have a closer look.'

'Be careful,' Pepe warned.

Heart in mouth, I inched around the tent. The cables seemed to all lead to one particular spot, where the dark turned deepest black. I blinked, my eyes adjusting.

There it was.

Set into the mountainside like a cave was the entrance to Tutankhamun's tomb. Despite all the newspaper headlines, all the gossip and stories buzzing around the world, it looked disappointingly ordinary. Just as Lysandra had described it, in fact, a tomb that didn't stand out or seem particularly royal.

There was a gate fastened across it – a wooden one, padlocked, which made it look rather like a coal bunker or a garden shed. Lysandra had told us about the rushed, shabby burial, and Maya storming off in disgust. I could see why. Even though Mr Carter must've put this gate here, it still felt sad and strange to have a person's grave under lock and key.

I moved a few steps closer. And a few more. The others were behind me in the shelter of the tent, too far away to call to. I supposed myself very alone. So when I heard voices again it caught me completely off guard.

'We're *looking*, remember, that's all,' said a woman.

I froze.

'Do you have the key, Pecky?' asked Mr Carter,

whose voice I knew instantly and who clearly wasn't at the cocktail party at all.

'Here.' A jingle of metal. The shuffling of feet on grit, and four people came out of the shadows to stand at the top of the steps to the tomb.

'Not a word of this to anyone, remember. If it gets out we've been here, we'll lose our permit entirely,' Mr Carter said.

They weren't officials or guards. They were Howard Carter, Lady Evelyn, a smaller, older man I recognised as Lord Carnarvon, and the person called Pecky with the key, whose silhouette was as huge and wide as a tree.

I dropped to the ground. Not that there was anything to hide behind: I was out in the open. And if I could see Mr Carter's group, then all it'd take would be a glance over their shoulders and they'd see me.

Oz was right; their torch had given up. Instead, the man called Pecky lit a kerosene lamp. Four faces huddled round it, all yellow-cheeked and shadowy. Once the gate across the tomb was open, they went inside, or rather, clambered in; the passage they disappeared into was still ankle-deep in rubble. All I could see now was the flicker of the lamp against bare walls. I glanced behind me to where Tulip and the others waited. Now was my chance to get back to them without being seen. But Grandad would want to know what Howard Carter was up to – and so did I. I crept towards the tomb.

From inside came a muffled banging noise: something fell to the ground. It sounded like a wall being knocked down. I inched even closer. What *were* they doing in there?

The banging stopped.

'This is where they broke in centuries before. Look, you can see where they patched up the hole,' said a loud, jolly voice that I assumed was Pecky's.

'Robbed in antiquity, eh? Just like the rest of the tombs here.' This was Lord Carnarvon, sounding annoyed. 'What if we open this up tomorrow, with everyone here, and find nothing but a few old pots inside? We'll be a laughing stock!'

'That's why we've come, Papa,' said Lady Evelyn. 'We're just going to check, that's all. We have to know it's not been plundered.'

There were more knocking sounds. Something heavy was being moved.

'If we take out those stones . . .'

'There, that's big enough to climb through . . .'

'You try first, Eve, you're the smallest.'

I couldn't believe they were going in, without any

permission to do so. I supposed that made them almost tomb raiders themselves. If what Pepe said was right, then they'd certainly be so in the eyes of Egyptian law.

Yet part of me couldn't blame them. I mean, who wouldn't – after all that digging and money spent, all those hopes and dreams – want to have a sly, secret look at what they'd discovered? Tomorrow, in daylight, it would all be official. Maybe tonight, when they thought they were alone, they could pretend what they'd found was theirs.

Hadn't I felt that too, that night in my bedroom when I'd unwrapped the jar for the first time? What about Grandad and Professor Hanawati when they'd seen it on a market stall? They knew the jar was valuable, and they'd wanted it for themselves.

So imagine being the first person inside the burial chamber for thousands of years. The last feet to have taken those steps would've probably been Lysandra, Ay and the rest of Tutankhamun's mourners. The thought made me dizzy.

Inside, Mr Carter called for another lamp.

'What can you see in there?' Lord Carnarvon asked.

I shuffled forwards till I was at the very top of the steps, holding my breath, waiting for the answer.

Mr Carter laughed. A great, thunderous, disbelieving laugh.

'Carter, tell me, can you see anything?' Lord Carnarvon insisted again.

'Yes.' Mr Carter sounded choked. 'Wonderful things.'

I clenched my fists, fighting the urge to run down the steps and have a look myself, and blow the consequences. But I knew already what was in that chamber: Lysandra had told us, so I could see it in my head. Chariot wheels, statues, swords, jewellery and baskets, which Mr Carter and co. were gazing at now in absolute amazement. Little did he know the room might well have been a dumping ground for the palace's unwanted things. Maybe it didn't matter: Lysandra's junk was his treasure. That seemed to be how history worked, sometimes.

As if to prove the point, from inside the tomb, someone squealed with delight. I was almost envious of Mr Carter, then. His dream had come true: he'd finally found what he'd been looking for all these years.

The curse hadn't put him off. He didn't fear that 'death would come on swift wings' to anyone who touched the pharaoh's tomb.

But then he didn't seem the type to be scared of anything. Nor did he have a desperately sick grandfather or a best friend with a scorpion sting. He hadn't read Lysandra's account, either.

Anyway, I reminded myself, we weren't here to take from a dead boy's tomb: we were here to put something back.

Frantically, I waved to the others behind the tent. With Carter inside gloating over his treasures, we could break our cover. Oz came out first, scuttling low like a spider. Then Pepe, leading the camels, with Tulip on Chaplin's back.

'Carter's inside the tomb. They've broken in,' I whispered once they'd reached me. Tulip and Pepe looked shocked.

'How on earth did he manage that? Where are the guards?' Tulip gasped.

'Money.' Pepe rubbed his fingers again. 'He'll have bribed them to keep quiet.'

'Well, he's in there now, so this is our chance to start climbing,' I said urgently.

Pepe tipped his head back to gauge the cliff. 'Straight up from *here*?'

I nodded. 'Can we leave the camels behind?'

'No. Both your suggestions are –' Pepe tapped the side of his head – 'cuckoo.'

I glared at him, but then I caught sight of Tulip's leg:

it wasn't realistic for her to walk anywhere, or climb. The swelling wasn't just in her foot any more, but had spread halfway up her calf.

Desperate, I turned to Pepe. 'We need to find a way up there. Is there a path?'

He thought about it for a nerve-rackingly long moment. 'I have local knowledge of the area, yes. Follow me.'

He walked steadily, his light-coloured *galabiya* visible in the dark. That would also make us easy to spot, so it was a relief when we rounded another heap of stones and were finally out of sight of the entrance to Tutankhamun's tomb. The trouble was, Pepe kept walking. The part of the cliff we needed to climb was getting increasingly far behind us.

'Um, Pepe?' I spoke up. 'Where are we going?'

He stopped to point to our left, where the valley side towered above us. In the dark, it was just an outline against the sky, but it did look slightly less terrifying than the other way. 'You can climb quickly, or you can take the camel way around.'

We had to trust him.

Yet even this route got tricky. The climb was so steep, we soon had to get off the camels and lead them – apart from Tulip, who clung to Chaplin's neck.

All too quickly, I was stupidly out of breath. Either side of the path was loose shingle. Sometimes, bits would fall on us from higher up the cliff.

'Ouch!' Oz yelped more than once. 'That hurt!' It did too, like someone with a pea-shooter was firing down on your head.

We'd been climbing for over an hour, when Tulip vomited. She did it very neatly over Chaplin's shoulder, and then insisted she was fine. She didn't sound it, mind you. I was anxious she was getting worse, and again I thought that we should've taken her back to the boat. It was too late now.

The path got even narrower the further we climbed. Under my satchel, my blouse was stuck to me with sweat. Our little rest stops soon started to become more frequent. Oz kept asking for water. Tulip told him to be quiet.

'How much further to the top?' I asked anxiously.

'Not far,' Pepe assured me. 'You can almost see it from here.'

You couldn't, but it was kind of him to lie.

When we set off again this time, the path looped back on itself. I started to feel more optimistic. At least now, I guessed, we were heading back in the direction of Mr Carter's dig. It was a hard climb, though. We went zig-zag fashion across more of the shingle, which was horrid stuff to walk on: it kept shifting and sliding away from you like loose snow. The camels, with their huge plate-like feet, managed it better than we did, though they didn't much like it when little stones from higher up the hillside started falling on us again.

'Arrggh!' Tulip cried, as one pinged off her cheek. Her camel lurched forwards like he'd been stung by a whip. Luckily, Pepe was leading him and quickly calmed him. Oz and I were holding Charlie, the sensible one, who just grunted and flicked his ears.

The stones kept raining down on us – nasty little things that hurt like anything – and I was worried the whole hillside was about to slide out from under our feet. Something higher up the path seemed to be disturbing the shingle.

Pepe, who'd stopped and was squinting upwards, clearly had the same idea. 'Oh dear me. I believe we've been spotted by a guard.'

'What? Where?' Following his gaze, I glimpsed a shoulder, a swinging arm, heard the crunch-crunch of footsteps. Someone was on the path above us.

'And there's a little detail I didn't tell you,' Pepe confessed. 'The guards here carry guns.'

19

'Guns?' My jaw dropped. 'What, with bullets and everything?'

'They are loaded, yes,' Pepe said quietly.

I glanced at Tulip, at Oz. I'd already put them through enough: this was extra danger we didn't need.

'What do we do now?' Tulip whispered.

Pepe raised a finger. 'Be quiet!'

I did, on tiptoe, straining my ears. The guard's footsteps above us got fainter, stopped, started again, then thankfully were gone. All I could hear was the desert. It wasn't like being down by the river, which buzzed with insects and people. Up here, where there was nothing but rocks and sand, the silence made your ears hum. I'd never known quiet like it, though that wasn't what Pepe meant.

About two hundred feet below us lights appeared once more. I was relieved to see how close we now were to the official tomb of Tutankhamun. Pepe's route had almost brought us back to the spot we'd started from, only this time we were seeing the Carter dig from above.

'They're coming out of the tomb!' Oz hissed. 'Are they carrying any loot?'

'I can't see anything obvious.'

'It's not theirs to take,' Pepe reminded us.

'Death shall come on swift wings,' Tulip murmured.

Yet none of the group looked remotely spooked or worried. Even from up here, I could sense their excitement. Mr Carter had an arm around Pecky's shoulders, Lady Evelyn had taken her hat off and was holding her head like she was stunned.

When the group finally mounted their donkeys and tottered away across the sand, I took a long slow breath. Now it was our turn.

'What about the guard?' Oz was worried. 'He's still out there somewhere. There might be more than one, you know.'

I glanced at Tulip, who was crouched low on her camel, shivering.

'We'll have to risk it.'

*

A few minutes later, we arrived at the very top of the cliff. There was no sign of anyone else up here. It was more bare rock, more sand. What we now had to do was find which way was east. By my reckoning it had to be at least two or three o'clock in the morning, if not later. Mrs Mendoza would be back from her cocktail party. If she was anything like my mum she'd be fretting herself silly about where we'd gone, but it was best not to think about that now.

'To find east,' Oz told me, 'you look at the stars.'

The trouble was, there were so many. Oz was scratching his head, looking confused. 'That's Venus, there. No, wait, it might be that one. Or is it Jupiter?'

'Ask Pepe,' I told him.

Meanwhile Tulip had slid off her camel and was peering intently at something on the ground. She picked it up, holding it suspiciously at arm's length. 'Look at this.'

It was a notebook, like the ones Mrs Mendoza used, covered in that funny dots-and-dashes writing reporters did incredibly quickly. It wasn't wrinkled or dirty, either. Someone must've only recently dropped it.

'That man we saw just now – it's got to be his,' Tulip said excitedly. 'I wonder if he's been watching Howard Carter too.'

'You think he's a reporter? Not a guard?' I asked, hopefully, because it'd mean we weren't about to get shot at least.

Before she could answer, Tulip threw up all over Oz's shoes.

After that she agreed to lie down. In the shelter of a heap of rocks, Pepe made her a pillow from his scarf. Chaplin, who I think had taken a shine to Tulip, dropped down nearby. Charlie stayed standing, swishing his tail like he was in very deep thought.

Together, we worked out where Venus was in the sky.

'Sunrise will be in an hour or so,' Pepe seemed to think.

Oz, shoeless and rather miffed, admitted Pepe knew more about stars than he did.

Once we'd found east, we started looking for a tomb entrance. I still had in my head the official one we'd seen down in the valley, which was set into the rock like a bunker. Back in England, Grandad had also shown me pictures of the Rameses tombs whose entrances were wider than the front door at the Winter Palace.

But we weren't looking for an official tomb, I reminded myself. We were searching for something so small and quiet it might easily be mistaken for a hole in the hillside or the resting place of an ordinary boy.

There was a ledge that ran just below the top of the cliff for ten, maybe twenty yards. In daylight, the views out over the valley from here would probably be terrific. It was as good a place as any to look, though at first glance there was nothing there – just more rock. More boulders to step around.

Behind me Pepe said something I didn't catch.

'Sorry?' I turned around a bit too fast. My right foot slipped off the ledge. Arms whirling, I fought to keep my balance. But everything was in the wrong place and there was nothing to hold on to but air. I panicked.

'Grab the rock!' Pepe yelled, waving frantically at a boulder that stood between us.

Just as I felt myself toppling over the edge, I latched on to it. First with one arm. Then the other. I squatted, hugging the boulder for dear life. When I finally felt safe enough, I fumbled to check my satchel was still there: it was, thank goodness.

It was then I felt air against my cheek. It came from behind the boulder – just once – and was warm, like someone's breath. I was also aware of a shift inside of me. As if my head was clearing, or I'd just stretched my tired legs.

No, that wasn't it. Not quite.

It was the absolute opposite of the gloomy, heavy

feeling I'd dragged around ever since Grandad fell ill. When Lysandra guessed what Maya had done with Kyky's heart, she'd said it was like a lock opening. It was the best way I could think of describing it too.

'Pepe?' I said, trying to stay calm. 'Can you come here a sec?'

We were more careful this time. Oz was under strict instructions to keep way back from the edge. The boulder wasn't much bigger than a motorcar tyre, but it took both Pepe and me to move it even a little way. Behind it was an opening. It was small – cupboard-door sized, probably. We crouched around it, trying to peer inside. But when I reached in with my arm I couldn't feel the end of it, and if anything, it seemed to get wider further along.

'It's the size for one person,' Pepe said.

'I'm the smallest,' Oz pointed out.

'And the youngest,' I reminded him. 'Your sister would go berserk if anything happened to you.'

'Aren't we a team?' he asked, sounding upset.

I looked at him. He was standing just back from the ledge, big-eyed, springy-haired. The boy who never went to school or spoke to strangers, here on a mountainside in Egypt in the middle of the night. He still wasn't one for hugs, mind you, so I patted his arm. 'We are a team,'

I told him. 'None of us would've done this on our own.'

He sniffed. 'But—'

'Sssh,' I stopped him. 'This last bit I'm doing for my grandad, all right? Stay with your sister. I won't be long.'

Hands stuffed in his pockets, Oz picked his way back along the ledge.

Pepe, though, didn't.

'I haven't enquired till now what exactly you are doing, English girl,' he said, folding his arms. 'But the time has come for me to ask.'

All I did was open my satchel and take out the jar. Even though it was still dark, I sensed the jar's power, its gleam of gold, the Anubis head, the heavy, important weight of it.

Twenty-two years ago, an Egyptian boy had stumbled across Kyky's tomb and the jar inside it. Very soon he regretted what he'd found. And out of nowhere, I thought of what Dad had said that day I'd stood up for Tulip in school.

Being English didn't give me the right to sort out other people's problems, not when they could solve them themselves.

'Here.' I handed the jar to Pepe. 'We're returning it to where it belongs.'

He did look amazed, I'll give him that. Even more

so when I mentioned what was inside, wrapped in old linen, and what Lysandra had told us about the boy pharaoh whose official tomb Mr Carter was feverishly exploring directly below us in the valley.

For a very long moment, Pepe held the jar to his chest.

'His *heart*?' he murmured, like he couldn't quite believe it, and who could blame him? When he'd recovered, there was a new determination in his face. He tucked the jar inside his gown.

'Let's begin,' he said and, crouching down, climbed in through the opening.

I followed. Crawling inside was the easy bit. I went on my belly, using my elbows, until the passage was wide and tall enough that I could get up on my hands and knees. Pepe must've gone fast because I lost him immediately. The quiet in here was thicker even than the quiet outside. All I could hear was the blood thumping in my ears. I was shaking a little – from tiredness, from the unbelievable thrill that this was it. I was here.

Then I got my first surprise. I expected the passage to keep going horizontally into the hillside. It didn't.

'Whoa!' I was falling.

Not far, thankfully. I landed with a jarring *thump* on

what felt like a step down. With my outstretched foot I could feel more steps cut into the rock. It was then, a little way below me, I saw a light.

'Pepe?' I called out.

'It's me,' he answered. 'These steps are risky. Here, have the torch.'

As Oz would've predicted, the torch was on the blink. There was just enough dim light to see steps spiralling downwards, though not in the logical way a staircase would: these took you by surprise. Pepe was just ahead of me, treading slowly and carefully. It took every ounce of my concentration not to stumble into him. Some of the steps were shallow, some deep; one was so far from the next that you had to leap to get to it. By the time we reached the bottom, my legs felt like string.

The torch went out.

The darkness was thick and total – not spooky, exactly, but rather queer. The air felt thick and stuffy, the walls a bit too close on all sides.

'We're burying the jar *here*?' Pepe whispered, sounding unsure.

Doubts, as doubts do, chose their moment, and suddenly my head was full of them. What if this *wasn't* the right place? Was I too late? Had Grandad already died? Was Tulip about to? Were the bad omens going to come true?

Tulip would have told me to pull myself together. Mum would have reminded me I had Grandad's spirit, and Dad, well, he'd have said our hard work had paid off. My brain, for once, listened.

'Yes,' I said. 'This is the place.'

A rustle of cloth as Pepe dug into his pocket. I sensed he now held the jar in his hands. When it started giving off a low, golden light, I thought it was just me imagining it. And maybe I was. Yet the glow got stronger. Not quite a torch beam, this was softer, more warming. It lit up Pepe's face. He said something in a language I didn't know.

As the light grew stronger, we could see we were in a little chamber. The floor was sandy, the walls curved on all sides – not bare rock, but decorated faintly with little figures and flowers. Open-mouthed, I turned slowly to take it all in. With a little bit of light, the tomb was beautiful.

In front of us was an arch that led to another chamber, above it a picture of a person in white robes, sitting on a throne. On his head the familiar tulip-shaped hat, the skin on his face blue. He was Osiris, god of the underworld who, Grandad once told me, was killed by someone in his own family who wanted to take his throne. How fitting to find his picture here, in Kyky's tomb.

There were other pictures – jackals, owls, cobras. To be truthful, I'd seen fancier ancient art back home in the British Museum, yet I'd never felt like this just from looking at it. Seeing it here, in Egypt, where it was supposed to be, meant something deeper – a connection, a sort of tingling in my chest. There was no gold, no lapis – apart from what Pepe held in his hands. I wondered what Mr Carter would make of this little place, whether if he saw it now he'd think it important enough to dig up and document. But then, maybe that was the point.

The tomb was private. It was the burial place for a beloved friend. What I really hoped most of all was that when Pepe and I climbed the steps out of here, no one would ever come down them again.

Yet one thing didn't add up: Maya said he'd chosen the spot for its position, because it would catch the sun. I couldn't think how any sun would ever get in here.

What caught my eye now was the arch below the Osiris drawing. Looking closer, I saw it wasn't a separate chamber at all, but two stone shelves running vertically into the rock. On each was a shape wrapped and wrapped again in cloth.

My throat tightened as I moved closer, the light from the jar growing ever brighter. As Pepe angled it towards the shelves, I could see what was, in fact, the top of a head. The shape of the body – the shoulders, the waist, the place where the feet would be – was just about visible under the fabric. Another mummified body lay on the shelf below. They were Lysandra and Maya, I felt sure of it.

'Are there people buried here?' Pepe asked in a hushed voice.

'Yes, they were all friends.'

I started to cry.

I'd expected the tomb to be just for Kyky's heart, but how stupid of me: without a decent family, his friends *were* his heart. I knew how that felt – not that my family weren't decent, but friends can be as important. And tears aren't always sad, either. Sometimes – like now, for instance – they could be a tangle of all sorts of feelings.

Very gently, Pepe put the jar on the top shelf. This mummy was the slightly bigger of the two, so I guessed it was Maya. The jar seemed to agree – if jars can do that. The light dimmed a little. It flickered, and then, with a fizzing, spitting sound, went out.

We waited. I didn't know exactly what I expected to happen, but I didn't think, somehow, that this was the end. The dark pressed in again, but only for a moment.

I blinked, stunned, as the whole chamber filled to the brim with light. This time it came from above, from the sky. Maya's measurements had been absolutely spot on. The first beams of the sunrise poured into the cave. It hit the far wall where the bodies lay. For a minute, or maybe for always, the three friends were together in the sun.

20

When we crawled out on to the ledge again, it was dawn. After dragging the boulder back into place, we sat against the cliff, exhausted.

'It went well,' Pepe said.

I looked sideways at him. 'It did.'

He nodded: we left it at that because I was crying, and so was he.

The sun was coming up over the valley. Where the light caught the tops of the hills, the rock looked almost pink. Everything else was in shadow – the road twisting along the valley floor, the boulders that marked the way. I'd never seen a view more beautiful, or more empty.

I wiped my eyes. Now, at last, the curse should be broken. We could start hoping for better, happier things.

I fancied a moment just to sit, and take it all in. I was so tired. But it was a good tiredness, like Nefertiti on a winter's evening curled up in front of the fire. After a while, Pepe left me to check on the others, but was back again in moments, looking agitated. Remembering Tulip, I scrambled to my feet.

'She's not worse, is she?' I asked.

He beckoned: 'Come. You can see for yourself.'

I followed him almost blindly off the cliff, back to the place where we'd left Tulip lying on Pepe's scarf. My heart was hammering. I didn't know exactly what to expect, but it certainly wasn't *three* people, where earlier there'd just been two.

Tulip looked better, thank heavens. Oz was beside her, staring not at his sister but at the new addition to the group, a blond-haired young man. All three were sitting cross-legged on the ground, the camels behind them dozing.

Tulip waved. As I approached she shot me a quick questioning look: *have you done it? Is the jar back where it belongs?*

I nodded.

Immediately, she was all smiles. 'Then you'll never guess who came back for his notebook?' It wasn't exactly hard to: the reporter was right there in front of me.

I stopped mid-stride. He looked *very* familiar. The

beard was gone, but the nice smile made me realise he was the man from the train.

'Crikey!' I said, grinning back. 'Hullo! Fancy you being here!'

'Hullo.' The man ran a hand rather sheepishly through his hair. 'I expect you've guessed who I am by now, haven't you?'

'Um ... well ... you seem to be a reporter ...' I offered.

As I sat down beside Tulip, I was aware of how shivery she was, not from fever any more, but with excitement. And Oz, who never looked directly at anyone much, was gazing at the young man like he was a Christmas present that might be snatched away from him at any moment.

'This is my best friend Lil,' Tulip said, then gestured to the reporter. 'And *this* is Alex.'

I stared at her. At him. At Oz. And at Pepe, who watched us, an arm round each of his camels' necks, tears still rolling down his face.

'Alex?' I frowned. 'What, as in your brother, Alex?'

'I don't think we've got another one!' Tulip laughed.

I was knocked sideways. This young man didn't look anything like the boy with the floppy hair whose portraits hung in the Mendozas' library.

'You got on the train in Yugoslavia! You're the second-class ticket man!' I cried. 'But your beard—'

'Gone,' he said, patting his face. 'It didn't suit me much, did it?'

He certainly looked better without it.

I turned to Oz. 'Blimey! This was who you saw at Athens station!'

But Oz, who'd normally have enjoyed being right, wasn't even listening. He had his brother back, the lucky devil – Alex, who was sitting there, with his notebook in his lap.

'So you're a reporter?' I said again, because it hadn't all sunk in.

'I'm afraid I am,' Alex admitted. 'I write for the *Washington Post*. I was sent by—'

'Mr Pemberton,' I finished. It all began to make sense. 'You're here to replace the man who had a motorcar accident in Italy.'

'That's it,' Alex nodded.

I was still confused. Where had he been since the war? Everyone in Tulip's family thought he was dead. But it wasn't my place to ask, I was learning this too. Sometimes people only told you things – difficult things – when they were ready to do so.

'Well, you know your mother's going to eat you for

breakfast, don't you?' I remarked.

Oz looked very worried. Tulip laughed fondly.

'I'm certainly going to get a proper telling-off, and I probably deserve it,' Alex agreed.

'I think we're all in for one of those,' I pointed out. 'But you being here, I mean, it's incredible.' And it was, though it didn't quite sink in that such a better, happier thing had happened already. All I could do was burst into a fresh bout of tears.

*

Mrs Mendoza was waiting for us with a face like thunder.

'I've just reported you all missing to the local police!' she cried, as we arrived back at the houseboat. 'Tulip, what on earth has happened to your leg?'

'It's better than it was last night,' Tulip told her.

When Mrs Mendoza saw Alex, the leg was forgotten. Yet she didn't come any closer. Maybe she didn't believe this person really *was* her son. Or maybe she was angry. We all stood on deck, not knowing what to say or do. The silence was agony. Alex, meanwhile, grew paler by the second.

'Here.' Tulip offered him a seat. As he sank into it, she settled herself protectively at his feet.

Oz moved his chair to sit next to his brother, the bond between them obvious. I felt glad for them, I really did. But this was family business. I was an outsider looking on: theirs was a team I wasn't part of.

In broad daylight, Alex's scars were more vivid. His hair tumbled forwards into his eyes once or twice, which made me think maybe he didn't look so different from the boy in the portraits after all. He was, I supposed, rather handsome. He also seemed very lost.

'Might we have some tea and toast, Mama? I'm starving,' Tulip suggested.

Mrs Mendoza went very white, then very red. 'You can't just walk in and expect *breakfast*!' She looked pretty scary, to be honest. Tulip seemed to recognise the look too: she looped her arm tighter around Alex's ankles.

'The war ended, Alex. They told us you were missing, believed dead.' Mrs Mendoza's voice was dangerously quiet.

Alex wiped his hands on his trousers. Even from where I was sitting I could see how much he was shaking.

'I was in a hospital in France, Mama. This scar on my face?' He touched it. 'Shrapnel. I couldn't speak, feed myself or remember anything for months. I didn't know who I was.'

I wished Mrs Mendoza would go to him and hug him, but all she did was close her eyes for a moment.

'Why didn't you come home when you'd recovered?' she asked in the same tight, quiet voice.

'Come home for what?' Alex asked. 'Look at me, Mama! I can't even hold a cup of tea without spilling it.'

Mrs Mendoza gritted her teeth. 'We thought you were dead. Everyone – even the War Office – thought you were dead.'

Alex was crying.

'I couldn't come home to you in pieces, Mama. You'd have been so disappointed.'

'*Disappointed?*' Mrs Mendoza looked shocked. 'You've never disappointed me, ever!'

I thought of all the silver cups on the library shelves, the place at Oxford. Alex's spectacular future was all mapped out for him.

'That's exactly it, don't you see?' Alex said. 'I'm not your dazzling boy any more. I've seen terrible things, seen chaps who I've shared lunch with die half an hour later. The war changed me.'

A lump grew in my throat as I thought of my dad. The war probably changed him too, though he'd never have said so much out loud. But hearing Alex give words and feelings to the sadness helped me understand a little better why Dad rarely smiled.

Mrs Mendoza, though, wasn't moved. 'Do you think you're the only person in the world who's suffered? All those wives who lost husbands, all those children without fathers, mothers without *sons*.' She almost spat the last word. 'And those men who did come home – disfigured, injured, out of their minds – do you think they found it easy? Do you?'

Alex shook his head.

'I lost two tiny babies before you came along,' she told him. 'You were my blessing. And then, four years ago, I thought I'd lost you too.'

It was getting harder to listen. Everything they were saying made me think of my parents, especially that Sunday afternoon in St Mary's churchyard. My mum had lost a baby, I'd never had the chance to be a sister to my brother, and all these years Grandad had missed out on having a grandson. In my family, it wasn't the dead people who were mourned, it was the living one we'd never got to know.

'I'm sorry.' Alex held up his hands. 'But the longer I stayed away, the harder it got to come back.'

When Mrs Mendoza stepped towards her son, I honestly thought she was going to hit him. She didn't; she hugged him at last. It was a fierce, bone-crushing embrace, and anyone could see how much she meant it.

*

Afterwards, we did have tea and toast.

'Where have you been all this time, Alex?' said Mrs Mendoza, adding sugar to our tea. Now her anger had eased a bit, she looked completely dazed.

'America, mostly. I gave up on history.' He smiled wryly. 'I'd had enough of dead people. I wanted to be a writer like you, Mama. I thought it might help me make sense of the world.'

Her face softened a little. 'And why are you here now? Did you track us down, or is it mere coincidence?'

'A little of both,' he said, taking a deep breath. 'You see, I followed in your footsteps ... I work for the *Washington Post*.'

I braced myself as Mrs Mendoza froze mid sip of tea.

Nervously, Alex hurried on. 'When my colleague had an accident, I was sent to cover this terrific story. It was my first big break. I leapt at the chance, of course. More than anything, I wanted to do it to impress you, don't you see?'

'You!' Mrs Mendoza nearly choked. 'Mr Pemberton sent *you*!'

'Oh lordy,' Tulip muttered under her breath. 'Here we go.'

I winced. It was all about to come out – our cover-ups, the misunderstandings about who'd sent which telegram and when. We'd also booked tickets under someone else's account. In amongst that lot, we'd probably done something rather criminal.

Yet the great unravelling of more secrets didn't come – at least not then. Mrs Mendoza was too stunned to say anything, and Alex, now he'd started, couldn't stop. 'I'd heard rumours of tensions between Mr Carter and the locals here, though not much has been said in the papers about that so far.'

'Back home they're making him sound like a hero,' I agreed.

'Exactly.' Alex nodded vigorously. 'I followed him last night, when he took off into the desert. He and Lord Carnarvon were up to no good, I'm sure of it, but they were on donkeys and I was on foot, so by the time I caught them up I'd missed the real action.'

'It's a possible story lead,' Mrs Mendoza admitted. 'But you'd need to have all the details to write about it.'

I put down my teacup.

'We were there,' I said. 'I saw it happen up close. What do you want to know?'

21

The tomb-opening ceremony was scheduled for two o'clock that afternoon. Almost everyone else travelled by motorcar to the Valley of the Kings, but we asked Pepe, Charlie and Chaplin to take us. The Mendozas, I suspected, liked to make an entrance, and by camel was a fine way to do it. There was also the issue of Tulip's scorpion sting, which was healing, but the lower part of her leg was still numb. Most important of all, though, was Pepe. It didn't feel right to go without him.

'We are an independent country now, not a colony,' he'd explained to us. 'We shouldn't let this Englishman dictate what happens to Tutankhamun's tomb.'

I couldn't help but think he'd have liked my grandad very much.

Pepe was, of course, very keen to be in on our plan, though to call it such was a bit grand. Put simply, where Mr Carter was concerned, we each had our axe to grind. Mrs Mendoza and Alex wanted a fresh news story. Pepe was keen for more Egyptian involvement in the dig. Tulip, I think, fancied going to a ceremony, and Oz – well, he was happy just to be near his big brother. As for me, I kept thinking about Grandad and Professor Hanawati. They'd learned the hard way about taking things that weren't yours. It was time for Mr Carter to hear about it.

Returning to the desert under the hot afternoon sun was a whole different experience to being there in the dark. Tulip, who was now very much at home on Chaplin, took the reins, whilst I sat behind.

'He's really quite intelligent,' she told me. 'He understands his name and everything.'

As she chatted on about the weather and what camels ate for breakfast, you could see Chaplin's ears flick back and forth, like he was hanging on her every word.

None of us looked particularly smart or clean by the time we climbed down from our camels. In full view of everyone, we'd had to slither down the rocky hillside, with Pepe behind us yelling, 'Lean back!' at the top of his voice. So it was an entrance, all right, and not a very dignified one.

Down in the valley it felt hotter than ever. Overhead, the sun beat down and on all sides the rocks threw out heat like giant, dusty ovens. It wasn't the sort of place you'd choose to spend time in: even in daylight it had a strange, unsettling atmosphere. No wonder Maya had chosen the clifftops instead.

A small gathering of people stood under an awning at the top of the tomb steps. Mostly it was men in suits. I spied Pecky amongst them, and the frail figure of Lord Carnarvon himself. The few ladies wore white summer frocks that fluttered in the hot breeze. After the ceremony, there was to be a tea party. Over by the tent where we'd hidden last night, a table had been laid with a crisp table cloth and silver cutlery that shimmered in the heat.

'How civilised it all looks,' Mrs Mendoza murmured.

'Ah yes, today they've invited the police chief and the provincial governor.' Pepe nodded in the direction of the two other Egyptian men present.

'Someone's drawn Lord Carnarvon's coat of arms on that stone, look,' Tulip said, pointing at a rock that'd been propped up near the tomb steps. It reminded me of a house-name sign or a number nailed to a front door.

Pepe wasn't impressed. 'Oh, how your Englishmen like to make themselves at home.'

To my over-hot, overwhelmed brain, the whole event felt like a farce. Everyone was here for a first glimpse inside a tomb which had, in secret, already been opened. It was all very proper, very much above board. What happened here last night, though, definitely wasn't.

A barely recognisable Mr Carter then sidled up to Mrs Mendoza. Jacket buttoned, hair parted and oiled, he looked terribly smart as he shook her hand and thanked her for coming. He even leaned over to ruffle Oz's curls, which made him yelp in horror and Tulip pull a face.

Mr Carter was all smiles. 'I'm delighted you could make it, Madeleine, though I trust you've no notebook or recording equipment about your person?'

'Of course not.' Mrs Mendoza beamed back at him. 'I'm here as your guest, nothing more.'

Like Tulip, she was good at lying when she had to be. So was Pepe, who salaamed graciously to Mr Carter, despite what he must've been feeling.

'How *do* you know him, Mama?' Tulip asked once Mr Carter had moved on.

'Well, darling...' Mrs Mendoza hesitated. It was the first time I'd ever seen her blush. 'The silly man tried to woo me once with a ring so ancient-looking it certainly wasn't from Tiffany's.'

'Was it *stolen*?' I asked.

Mrs Mendoza adjusted her hat. 'Let's just say Mr

Carter has probably been helping himself to Egyptian gold for rather a long time. He's been worried I'll blow his cover ever since.'

Tulip made quiet little sick noises at the thought of her mum and Mr Carter. I had to admit, it was a bit disgusting.

But it was also a reminder – as if I needed one – that Mr Carter should know we had our eye on him.

Our attention was quickly drawn by an official clapping his hands and beckoning us over to the tomb entrance for the start of the ceremony.

Mr Carter was the first to speak: 'Ladies, gentlemen, dignitaries.' He gestured towards the tomb entrance, where last night's gate now stood wide open. 'Welcome to our latest discovery, KV62. K meaning Kings, V meaning Valley. It is the sixty-second tomb to be discovered here. Now, if you'd like to follow me.'

Tulip leaned on my arm as we made our way down the tomb steps.

'Just remember who else has walked here,' I said, thinking of Lysandra and her brother who would've been in this exact spot all those centuries ago. It was hard not to be a tiny bit thrilled.

'It's amazing, isn't it?' Tulip agreed. 'I keep thinking of everything Maya did for his friend.'

'That's what friends do,' I told her fondly, squeezing her arm. 'At least the very best ones.'

At the bottom of the steps, Mr Carter led us into a narrow passageway that sloped gently downhill. The air was warm and rather stale. After the bright sunshine, the lantern-lit gloom took a bit of getting used to.

The chamber wasn't exactly big – the fifteen or so of us soon filled it – but it was much larger than Kyky's tomb up on the cliff face. It felt different too, neat and impersonal, like a bed that no one had slept in.

When the passage came to an abrupt halt at another door, Tulip hissed in my ear, 'Get ready: it's show time!'

As fifteen people all jostled for a view, we found ourselves on tiptoe at the back. The door, though not particularly tall, was wide, covered in plaster and little seals that Mr Carter was saying now bore evidence of the tomb being a royal one. A basket and some reeds stood in front of the door: Mr Carter whisked both away to reveal a hole hastily patched up with wood and plaster.

'We're not sure yet if the tomb beyond this door is untouched. Grave robbers have been here in the past, as you can see,' he told us.

He had a nerve. We knew he'd knocked a hole

in the wall last night. So did Lord Carnarvon and his daughter. But they let Mr Carter weave his story anyway, dazzling us with lies.

'And now, ladies and gentlemen, in the presence of our Egyptian friends, we'll endeavour to break into the tomb.' Mr Carter motioned for a workman to come forward.

An excited murmur spread through the group as the man began prising off the nailed-on bits of wood. I watched in amazement. Surely *he'd* know those weren't ancient nails. The plaster would still be wet, the wood freshly cut. Nobody spoke up, though. The workman kept pulling, as Mr Carter, Lady Evelyn and Lord Carnarvon watched, as cool as a whole bunch of cucumbers.

Next we were invited to come and peer through the hole in the door. Being very English, we formed a queue, going up one at a time.

'Let the children go first,' someone said, and before we knew it, we were nudged to the very front of the line.

'It's Ay's old junk, remember,' Tulip whispered, as Mr Carter beckoned me to come forward.

'Ready, young miss?' he asked.

Everyone was watching: I could feel their eyes on me as I wiped my sweaty hands in my skirt. 'Yes.'

With a click, the torch went on, and he shone it into the dark inner room. The first thing I saw was a wheel, then a glorious-looking chariot lying on its side. I bit my lip in surprise: was it the chariot Kyky used to race Maya?

Seeing something I recognised from Lysandra's account took the wind out of me, rather. This tomb – big, golden, soon to be world-famous – was all for someone who'd once been a living, breathing, pomegranate-throwing young man.

As the beam swung left, it picked out a gold box, a sandal, a statue's eye, the pleats of a tunic. More objects glinted as the light moved. In a far corner were two black figures, both as tall as a man, standing either side of another door, like they were guarding it. I couldn't see a coffin, though, or anything that might be a mummified body. At my guess, this was just an outer chamber. The door in the corner might well lead on to more rooms like this one, heaped full of three-thousand-year-old treasure. It was an incredible find, there was no denying it. It was probably beyond even Mr Carter's dreams.

'There you are, then, that's enough,' he said, abruptly switching off the torch.

I rubbed my eyes, like I was waking up from a dream of my own. Mr Carter was already beckoning Tulip to take her turn, but I didn't move aside.

'Mr Carter, what are you going to do with all these things?' I said. My politest voice wasn't a patch on Tulip's but it got Mr Carter's attention.

'They'll be removed, cleaned up, recorded and catalogued,' he explained. 'Lord Carnarvon is a collector, the Metropolitan Museum in New York have an interest.' He stopped to frown. 'Why do you ask?'

There was a silence. Everyone stared at me. The two Egyptian officials who stood at the edge of the group were scowling. One of them looked away in obvious annoyance.

I could feel myself clamming up. I glanced at Tulip, then Oz, who was studying his shoes. It was Alex who mouthed: *Keep going!*

I straightened my shoulders.

'My grandad was a collector of sorts,' I said. 'He came here to Egypt over twenty years ago, and with a friend they bought something—'

'Charming, I'm sure,' Mr Carter interrupted, eyeing his wristwatch. 'Look, do you kids want to see inside the tomb or not? Other people are waiting to have a look, and then I've got a tea party to host.'

'Exactly.' This was Lady Evelyn. 'Do hurry up now.'

I still didn't move.

'Mr Carter, my grandad and his friend spent the rest

of their lives regretting taking the object that wasn't theirs. It should never have been removed from its tomb in the first place. Having it brought them all sorts of terrible luck. His friend has now died, and my grandad is gravely ill in hospital.'

'If this is about the curse, then it's tommyrot,' Mr Carter said, irritably. He pushed past me, but stopped in surprise as Tulip, Oz and Alex blocked him from going any further. 'What ruddy nonsense is all this, then?'

'We want you to listen,' Tulip said. 'It's not right to disturb dead people's tombs.'

Someone coughed. Over to my left I heard Lord Carnarvon mutter, 'Who the devil is this girl?'

Mr Carter meanwhile looked daggers at Tulip, then at me. 'Your grandad knows you're here, does he, giving me a headache?'

'I'll tell him all about it when I get home,' I replied sharply. 'He'd be proud of me.'

'Why, you cheeky little swine!' cried Mr Carter.

I didn't flinch. Mr Carter had overlooked who the tomb really belonged to. He'd talked round the Egyptians with his authority and powerful connections, but the other side to him – the secret, shabby, bloody-minded side – he'd kept hidden. He was, in that sense, a sun king.

'That time my grandad came to Egypt, he met you, Mr Carter,' I said, more sure of myself, now. 'He told me your job was to clear old tombs, and that you helped yourself to any objects that caught your eye.'

'I did no such thing!' Mr Carter looked horrified.

I pressed on. 'The locals didn't think much of how you went about your business, even then. But you just kept going, doing things your way. And woe betide anyone who stood up to you.'

'How dare you speak to your elders in such a way!' Lord Carnarvon exclaimed.

'But it's true,' I insisted.

'Is it?' Mr Carter squared up to me. 'What was he called, this grandad of yours?'

'Ezra Wilkinson,' I said looking him straight in the eye. 'And his friend was Professor Selim Hanawati.'

The angry mask slipped, just for a beat, then it was back, harder than ever. 'Never heard of either of them,' he snarled.

He was lying – badly. But I'd rattled him, which was oh so satisfying. So was the look on Mrs Mendoza's face: she was taking in every word.

'Before you go, Mr Carter,' I called out, as he tried to barge past Tulip, 'we saw you here last night, the four of you breaking into the tomb.'

There was a gasp. A shaking of heads in the crowd. A few mutterings of 'Oh I say!' under people's breaths. Best of all were the Egyptian officials, one of whom folded his arms in a very satisfied way. The other smoothed his moustache, then took a long breath like he was readying himself for battle.

Mr Carter himself spun round, furious. 'Claptrap! We weren't anywhere near the place! What sort of mother lets you lot run wild in the desert at night? The police should hear about this.'

'And you should've had an official from the government with you,' Oz pointed out. 'Otherwise, you could've stolen more things that no one would ever know about.'

'Indeed, that is the law,' the moustachioed Egyptian man spoke up. 'I'm sure Mr Carter is very aware of this fact. Or perhaps he needs a little reminding that he is here at *our* invitation.'

By now Lord Carnarvon and Lady Evelyn were looking very agitated indeed. Since it was clear we weren't budging, they began trying to usher everyone outside.

Mr Carter glared at Oz: I honestly thought he was going to box his ears.

'*Did* you take anything, Mr Carter?' I asked.

'Because if you did, be warned: there is a curse. It's not tommyrot, not for a second.'

He turned his glare on me. Then he roared at the top of his lungs, so loud they must've heard him back in Luxor: 'I WILL NOT BE HELD TO RANSOM BY A GROUP OF CHILDREN!'

Tulip caught my eye. I smiled. We'd got him, beautifully.

PART FIVE

Everywhere, the glint of gold.

HOWARD CARTER, ARCHAEOLOGIST

22

The very next day, Mr Carter decided to 'put the record straight'. He offered Mrs Mendoza and Alex an exclusive interview, the only condition being that no children should be present. I was very glad to hear it: frankly, I'd had enough of his stories. In a hired room at the Winter Palace, Mr Carter came clean about what he called their 'preliminary viewing' of the tomb that night. He had, without meaning to, put a piece of ancient plasterwork in his jacket pocket. But that was all accounted for now, no harm done.

I imagined Mrs Mendoza and Alex furiously writing all this down in their notebooks. They were certainly pretty thrilled with their final story, which was wired not to Mr Pemberton at the *Washington Post* but to the *Cairo Gazette*. An Egyptian story deserved an Egyptian publication, Mrs Mendoza said.

Neither Lord Carnarvon nor Lady Evelyn took

part in the interview. The exclusive deal they were pushing for was with *The Times*. According to Pepe, though, the real reason was that Mr Carter and Lord Carnarvon had been arguing over how best to clear the tomb.

All their good fortune came at a price.

You see, nobody, not even Mr Carter, had expected the tomb to be *so* jammed full of treasure. Bizarrely, by being such a rushed, un-royal-looking grave, Tutankhamun's official resting place had remained untouched like no other tomb before it – not even Kyky's. Mr Carter was very confident that when they opened the inner chamber, they'd find the young pharaoh's remains intact.

We kept quiet about that.

Suffice to say the story in the *Cairo Gazette* made life difficult for Mr Carter. The call for more Egyptian involvement in the dig grew, and Mr Carter, stubborn as the donkeys he rode, locked the gate on the dig and declared the excavation season over until spring. Things were definitely not going to plan. Or, as Pepe put it, 'Tutankhamun's curse has turned its sights on Mr Carter at last.'

*

When Mrs Mendoza announced it was time for us to go home, I was both excited and apprehensive. I'd had no more news about Grandad, so I wasn't sure what exactly I'd find when I got to London. There were farewells to say, to three old friends now together in their little clifftop tomb, and to three new ones – Pepe, Charlie and Chaplin, who'd made me think about many things, including camels, in a whole different light. Tulip sobbed like a baby saying goodbye to Chaplin.

'I'll write,' she promised him. The look on Pepe's face was a picture.

On our very last evening, when everyone else had gone to bed, I stayed up on deck by myself. As I lay there, listening to the river lapping gently against the boat's hull, I heard a rustling coming from the reeds on the riverbank. I sat up just in time to see a dog creep to the water's edge. It was only a couple of feet away. Close enough to touch.

I could see it wasn't a normal dog. It was bigger and quieter than the mangy strays from the town, and its ears stuck up on the top of its head like the Anubis on Kyky's jar. I wondered if it might be a jackal. I *hoped* it was – it felt right that it should be, somehow.

As the jackal started drinking, I kept absolutely

still. Then it heard something in the distance and its head went up. It saw me watching it. For the tiniest moment, we stared right at each other, before it turned tail and vanished.

I'd like to think it was a sign that the gods of ancient Egypt were protecting Kyky. Despite all Mr Carter's digging and cataloguing, the real Tutankhamun finally was free.

*

Six and a half days later we were home. London was upon us all too quickly. In the suburbs we passed acres and acres of new houses being built. After Cairo, the view from the window as we came into St Pancras station was grey, cold, dreary. Yet there were Christmas lights twinkling prettily in all the shops, and a definite cosiness to all the lamp-lit windows and smoking chimney pots. Dear London: how I loved it. I was glad to be back.

Mrs Mendoza had wired ahead to say we were returning. And there they were, both Mum and Dad, waiting at the ticket barrier. They had on their best coats and hats, and their faces when they saw me coming made me well up with tears. I hesitated, though, when I spotted who else was there with them, wrapped up against the cold. Though he looked small and pale, it was definitely an improvement on when I'd last seen him in a hospital bed. Besides, I'd have known those twinkling blue eyes anywhere.

'Grandad!'

I ran the last few yards, suitcase thumping against my leg. Grandad reached out his arms and I went straight into them. I buried my face deep into his coat. He smelled of old things and Nefertiti.

'Oh, Lily!' He hugged me tightly, drew away to look at me, hugged me again. Hands patted my shoulders; I heard Mum say my name, then Dad clear his throat. We were all having a bit of a cry.

There were more hugs, hands being shaken as the Mendozas joined us at the barrier. In the hustle and bustle of it all, I noticed Grandad go very still. He'd been pale before, but now the colour completely went from his face. I panicked, thinking he was about to collapse or something.

'Do you need to sit down?' I asked him.

But, it wasn't that he was ill: he'd seen someone behind me, over my shoulder. I turned around, and there was Alex, looking every bit as startled himself.

23

Just because we'd broken the curse didn't mean the world made sense again. If anything, for a while at least, life got more complicated. One thing we did agree on was that St Pancras station with a ticket barrier wedged between us wasn't the place to discuss it, so we all went back to Grandad's instead.

As usual, we were greeted by Nefertiti, and a hallway full of carpets and boxes. Yet instead of taking us straight into the shop, Grandad ushered us upstairs to the front parlour. The last time he'd used this room was in 1918 when the war ended, so I knew he had something really important to tell us, which gave me the jitters all over again.

'I think everyone should sit down,' he said.

Wiping off the layers of dust, we perched on what chairs or stools we could find. Oz, who'd taken an immediate liking to Nefertiti, sat with her on the floor. From a drawer, Grandad took out an envelope with photographs inside, which Mrs Mendoza seemed to recognise straight away.

'That's my writing,' she cried in alarm.

Grandad placed a hand on his chest. 'I'm Ezra Wilkinson,' he explained. 'You've been sending me pictures of my grandson all these years.'

Her mouth fell open.

'And you're Mrs Mendoza,' he said to her. 'Or should I say, Mrs Fulbright.'

She nodded, looking worried. 'That was my first husband's name, yes.'

'Are you following all this, Lil?' Tulip whispered.

I gulped. 'I think so.' Though who knew that two families could be so complicated – and complicated *together*.

Certainly Mum seemed to grasp what was going on, because she'd got her hankie out and was dabbing her eyes.

Grandad laid out the photographs on the floor for us to see. They were all of a blond-haired boy, sixteen in total, one for each year as a child. He'd got them in date order, starting with a baby in knitted booties, then a toddler on a swing. At least half of the pictures showed the boy holding some sort of silver cup or certificate. The last was of a young man in army uniform: Alex.

It was ridiculous. Totally and utterly.

Yet when I glanced at Mum, she was shaking with tears. 'All these years you've been in touch and never told me?' she cried, staring at Grandad.

'My dear, I thought it for the best,' he replied, though he looked very unsure about it.

Dad kissed the top of Mum's head, telling her it would all be all right. Alex – *Tulip's* brother Alex – looked the most confused of any of us.

'Well,' he said, running a hand through his floppy hair. 'This is rather a surprise.'

'But you told me your baby was called Ezra,' I said to Mum.

'He was, Lil,' Mrs Mendoza answered for her. 'He still is. But we call him by his middle name – don't ask me why, it's always been that way.'

I felt dizzy. Ever since Mum had told me the secret, I'd been imagining where my brother might now be, and this past week or more he'd been right under my nose. It was really too bizarre to be true. But then, come to think of it, so was a pharaoh's curse and a three-thousand-year-old heart wrapped up in a jar. 'Ezra Alexander,' I said, though I couldn't begin to think what his surname might be. 'Gosh . . . I mean . . . I'm not sure how to say this, but do you mind being my brother?'

Alex puffed out his cheeks, shook his head, then smiled. 'Actually, Lil, I've been meaning to thank you for the glass of lemonade. You were kind to me that day when you didn't even know me. So I couldn't wish for a better, braver sister.'

Tulip grinned. 'I'll pretend I didn't hear that.'

Afterwards Tulip said I'd gone a very funny shade of grey, so I suppose it was the shock. And I was happy, I really *really* was, though happiness that huge takes a bit of getting used to.

*

But I did get used to it. Our little family suddenly felt stronger and bigger, not just with the addition of Alex, but the Mendozas too. And as I got to know Alex, it helped me understand Dad more and more. There was no denying how delighted he was to find his son, yet I also came to know the signs that showed he loved me just as much. All the pushing, the university talk, it was about wanting me to have the same opportunities, the same chances as any boy would have.

'When men try to change the world it ends up with fighting,' he said to me one day when we were on our own making supper. 'Girls like you and Tulip, you're the future. You'll use your brains to get things done.'

It changed the way I saw St Kilda's. So did the fact that Tulip now came to school, and Millicent Thorpe gave us both a wide berth, which made me wonder if Mrs Emerson-Jones had actually listened the day she birched me. Though nothing – and I mean, nothing – could ever make me like the stupid St Kilda's felt hat.

Alex, meanwhile, went back to living with the Mendozas, but came to us for his roast lunch every Sunday. Grandad would come along too, and Dad actually didn't mind. The arrival of Alex had healed their rift, which I suspected had, all along, been to do with the baby they'd given away. Perhaps if Grandad had been here and not in Egypt at the time, things would've worked out differently. We'd never know.

It was funny seeing us all together, squashed in our little kitchen. Alex, whose good looks I'd assumed came from Mrs Mendoza, was in fact a dead ringer for Dad. His blue eyes were the same shade as Mum's, and Grandad's, though Alex swore he looked just like me. I'd never thought of myself as this-haired or that-eyed, or whether I was half presentable in the face department, but even I knew that being likened to Alex wasn't going to be bad news, by anyone's stretch.

And when my parents sat in their chairs each night

by the fire, they looked different too. Like a weight had lifted, or a window had opened. They looked happier than they'd ever done.

*

It was at our kitchen table, a few months later, that I heard the latest report from Egypt.

'That poor man,' Mum muttered from behind the newspaper.

I assumed she meant Mr Carter, who'd made the headlines again recently when a bust of Tutankhamun was found hidden, all boxed ready as if someone was planning to ship it out of the country. He faced suspicion, it seemed, at every turn.

'Don't feel sorry for Mr Carter,' I said, finishing the last of my toast and getting up from the table. These days I walked the last bit of the route to school with Tulip, and didn't want to be late.

'It's not him this time, love.' Mum showed me the headline:

'PHARAOH'S CURSE CLAIMS CARNARVON.'

Underneath, I read the shocking news of Lord Carnarvon's death in Cairo. In weakened health anyway due to the stresses of the dig, he'd cut open a mosquito bite on his face whilst shaving. The bite got infected, and he'd died of a fever a couple of weeks later. It was a sad end to his big, expensive dreams. And strange how the bite sounded rather like the one Lysandra mentioned on Kyky's face.

In the news piece, much was made of the curse, and how random people – reporters, writers, an actress – had predicted Lord Carnarvon's death in the weeks beforehand. All because he'd disturbed a pharaoh's rest.

For most readers, it was probably a silly, sensational twist to a rather tragic story. But it sent a little warning shiver across my skin. Grandad, I supposed, might've got better anyway, though it wasn't a risk I'd ever wanted to take. We'd been right to fear the curse.

*

One Saturday, when life had settled into its new rhythms, I went to the British Museum with Tulip and Oz. It was a fine sunny day, so we decided on a picnic lunch. Oz, I noted, was wearing an enormous overcoat.

'It's so cold today,' he'd said, dramatically rubbing his arms.

It really wasn't. It was another of Oz's quirks, and I'd grown used to them by now. We were meeting

Alex, who'd recently got work in the Egyptian Rooms writing up Professor Hanawati's research findings. Since the professor's death, the museum had acquired most of his papers, including notes that documented his finds, though we were glad to know there was no mention of an Anubis-headed jar.

Waiting for Alex's lunch break to start, we strolled through the Egyptian Rooms. As ever, I felt at home here, and was glad that such places existed so we could learn about the world, and the people who'd lived in it. The gold breastplates, the clay pots, the mummified pets, all had stories that we could only guess at. That was part of the mystery. So were the things we'd never dug up, never seen. We didn't have to understand *everything*, at all costs.

There was plenty of our own stories we still didn't know. Like why Maya chose for the light to flood Kyky's tomb on that particular day. Or why Pepe had named his camels after a movie star. Or what was going on in Alex's mind when he went to America after the war instead of coming home. Even things like why the *Washington Post* never chased Mrs Mendoza for her travel expenses incurred on a trip for four to Luxor.

As Grandad himself would say, some things were best left alone.

Mr Carter didn't agree. In the Valley of the Kings, he'd now started emptying King Tutankamen's tomb in earnest. But after Lord Carnarvon's death his relationships with the Egyptians, already tense, got even trickier. Or maybe it was the curse having its final say.

The story, though, still captured people's imagination worldwide. *The Times*, its exclusive deal done, published pictures of treasures being carried out into daylight, and accounts of all the gold to come. Everyone knew about it. Talked about it. The Egyptian Rooms were busy like never before.

To me, it was still an intriguing tale. But now I was aware of a different side to it, it'd lost some of its shine. Knowing Kyky, Lysandra and Maya were at rest – that to me was the real story, and it was worth more than gold.

*

When Alex finally appeared for his lunch break, sandwich packet in hand, we agreed to go to Russell Square, where we hoped the grass would be dry enough to sit on. What's more, between us, we had a brilliant selection of sandwiches and cake – so tasty that even Oz couldn't resist a nibble. The reason for his huge overcoat also became clear when it started moving of its own accord.

I stopped chewing. 'I say, Oz, you haven't brought the cat along, have you?'

Nefertiti's head appeared by way of reply. We all pretended to be shocked, but the two had become pretty inseparable since that day in Grandad's front parlour. Oz had been going there regularly for tuition, which suited such a pair of history buffs very well indeed.

'Your grandad didn't mind,' Oz said. 'And Nefertiti certainly didn't.'

The picnic was soon gone, but the afternoon stretched before us, warm and lazy. Alex was the first to start gathering his things.

'Lunch hour's over. I'd better get back.'

'Stay another five minutes,' I pleaded.

'Yes, do,' agreed Tulip. 'It's too nice to be inside.'

Oz nodded. Nefertiti miaowed.

Alex grinned: 'All right. Five minutes it is.'

It'd taken a long, dusty journey to get to this moment. Sometimes, even now, I just had to pinch myself. If the ancient Egyptians were right, and this life was our practice run for the next, then that was fine with me. My heart was here, in its rightful place.

So we sat – friends, brothers, sisters and a Siamese cat – for a little longer, all together, with our faces turned to the sun.

AUTHOR'S NOTE

'Tutankhamun' is a name so famous it's tricky to do it justice. So much has been written about him, so many interpretations made as to who he was and how he met his fate. Even as I type, new theories about possible undiscovered chambers in his tomb are emerging. It's a story that keeps on fascinating us.

As a writer of historical fiction, I feel it's important to clarify that only some of what I've included in my story is documented fact. Tutankhamun's tomb was discovered by Howard Carter in late November 1922. Lord Carnarvon, Carter's patron, had agreed to fund one last dig, but died of an infected mosquito bite the following April before most of the tomb's contents were fully documented. His death fuelled rumours of a curse, which only made the Tutankhamun story more intriguing and alluring.

The timing of the tomb's discovery was extremely sensitive: Egypt had become an independent country in early 1922, yet British and American archaeologists and collectors were soon jostling for a claim on Tutankhamun's treasure. Howard Carter – stubborn, clever, determined – was known to be a difficult man. His relationship with the Egyptian authorities was strained, to say the least, and worsened after Lord Carnarvon's death.

Much of what is said about Tutankhamun and his tomb depends on whose accounts you read. Over the years, the pharaoh's mummy has been unwrapped, X-rayed, scanned. How exactly he died is still up for debate. Some say it was a chariot crash, others suggest he was murdered in a struggle for power. Evidence shows he had an injury to his head and leg. Very unusually for Egyptian burial rites, his heart had been removed. Tests also found him to have various strains of malaria.

This is where the *fiction* part of my story comes into play. As far as I know, Tutankhamen's missing heart has never been found, nor has an account of his last days as king. For pace, I have condensed down the events of November 1922. My Howard Carter is brash and rather untrustworthy. As far as I know, no children were present at the first 'opening' of the tomb. The time it took to travel across Europe to Luxor is based on accounts from the day and estimations.

My fictional narrator Lil takes her name from the very real Ella Lily Kaye, whose mum bid for her to be a named character in my next book, during the Authors For Grenfell charity auction last year. I hope my Lil lives up to her namesake.

Emma Carroll
May 2018

Q & A WITH EMMA CARROLL

Why did you decide to write a story about Ancient Egypt?

I've always been fascinated by Egyptology – the rituals, the religions, the way people lived their everyday lives. Until Howard Carter unearthed his tomb in 1922, Tutankhamun was considered a relatively minor pharaoh. Yet as the world struggled to recover from World War 1, Tutankhamun's story brought much-needed excitement and glamour, and captured the public's imagination in unprecedented ways. It was this – why people were so interested in the discovery of a long-dead young man – that intrigued me most of all.

How much research did you do?

I read books on Howard Carter, watched documentaries, trawled internet sites. In 1994, when I'd finished uni,

I went backpacking through Egypt. Some of the details in the book are taken from my own experiences. I did enough research to create – I hope – a believable world: things like clothes, food, living conditions, expectations, attitudes. Yet the story always comes first.

Many have dubbed you 'The Queen of Historical Fiction'. What is it that draws you to writing historical fiction?

I'm a massive fan of reading historical fiction, so that definitely influences what I write. For me, it's the world-building, the intriguing little customs, sayings, bits of social history that feel both familiar and strange, which make it such a great genre to write. I'd imagine it's similar to writing fantasy, only with more corsets and candlelight.

Who or what inspired the character of Lil?

Lil is named after Ella Lily Kaye, whose mum bid on the Authors For Grenfell charity auction for her daughter's name to feature in my next book. The character herself is my own creation. Lil's a girl very much of the era – on one hand she clings to the past and what she knows, but on the other hand, she's dying to face the new challenges that come her way.

How did you decide on the title of the book? Do you usually start with a title or does it come later in the process?

Originally the story was called 'The Lost Boy', which came to me very early in the writing process, as my titles tend to do. But we then realised quite a few other books had this same title, so I came up with the alternative.

The story has a feminist message – how important was this to the era?

Very. World War 1 meant women had to step into men's roles, often doing their jobs, managing households, money, etc. By the time the war ended, women had proved themselves as capable as men in all sorts of ways. In 1918, women over thirty years of age with property were able to vote. It was a step in the right direction, yet only accounted for 40 per cent of the female population. If you were young and poor, like Lil and her mum, your voice still wasn't heard.

Can you sum up the main themes of the book and how you chose these?

Recovery, secrets, putting right past wrongs, friendship, fitting in, having courage to swim against the tide. I wasn't aware of 'choosing' the book's themes. They grew with each draft of the story.

Things to Talk About

* Do you think Lil was right to open the package?

* Lil is sent to an all girls school. What do you think about this?

* Mrs Mendoza says the job of reporting on the discovery is 'a man's job'. Do you agree?

* Lil's Grandad believes that the jar is cursed. Do you believe that items can be cursed? What makes you reach your conclusion?

* 'It's not right, all this digging up the dead to make the living feel better.' Do you agree or disagree with this statement? Why?

* Lil follows her parents to see where they are going. Do you think this is ever OK?

* Lil is allowed to take time off school to go to Egypt. Do you think there are circumstances where it's fine for children to be off school?

* Who do the 'finds' belong to? Egypt or Howard Carter?

* Lil's father says that men change the world with fighting, where women use their brains. Do you think this is a fair statement? Why?

For more resources, head to:
www.faber.co.uk/faber-childrens-resources

Tell us what you think!
🐦 **@FaberChildrens #SunKing**

ACKNOWLEDGEMENTS

This story would still be half-finished on my laptop if it wasn't for the support, prodding and general cheerleading of the wonderful team at Faber Children's. Particular thanks go to my editor Alice Swan for knowing when to push and when to listen. Special mentions to my fantastic publicist Hannah Love, to Sarah Lough for clever, inventive marketing, and to the linchpin in everything, project editor Natasha Brown.

Faber is full of brilliant people – Emma Eldridge in design, Lizzie Bishop in rights, Kellie, Mel, Sam, John and the sales team. Julian De Narvaez continues to surpass himself with his cover illustrations. I am so lucky to work with you all.

I'm massively grateful to booksellers and librarians whose skill ensures books find the right readers. To bloggers, journalists, reviewers, you make such a difference to a book's exposure: thank you.

Huge thanks to the teaching community who've embraced reading with such enthusiasm. Your schools should be so proud of you. It's been a real joy to chat via Twitter and say hello to your students!

To Maz, Kiran, Maya, Perdita, Abi, Ross, Robin, Peter, James, and too many other fellow writers to mention. We look out for each other, and I love that.

And to all the readers who've sent letters, emails, or who've turned up at book signings and festivals, meeting you is the best part of being an author.

Finally, my nearest and dearest. For the phone calls I've forgotten to make, the headaches, the early starts, the being grumpy and begging you to look after my dogs while I go on yet another trip, I'm sorry. Most of all to my husband who, as I start the first draft of my next book, faces the process all over again. A heartfelt, gargantuan thank you.